The Winter Dress

Angela Keogh

The Harvest Press

The Winter Dress
By Angela Keogh
Published in 2020
by The Harvest Press
www.theharvestpress.ie

Copyright 2020 Angela Keogh
ISBN 978-1-8380836-1-8

Illustrations : Magda Noskowska

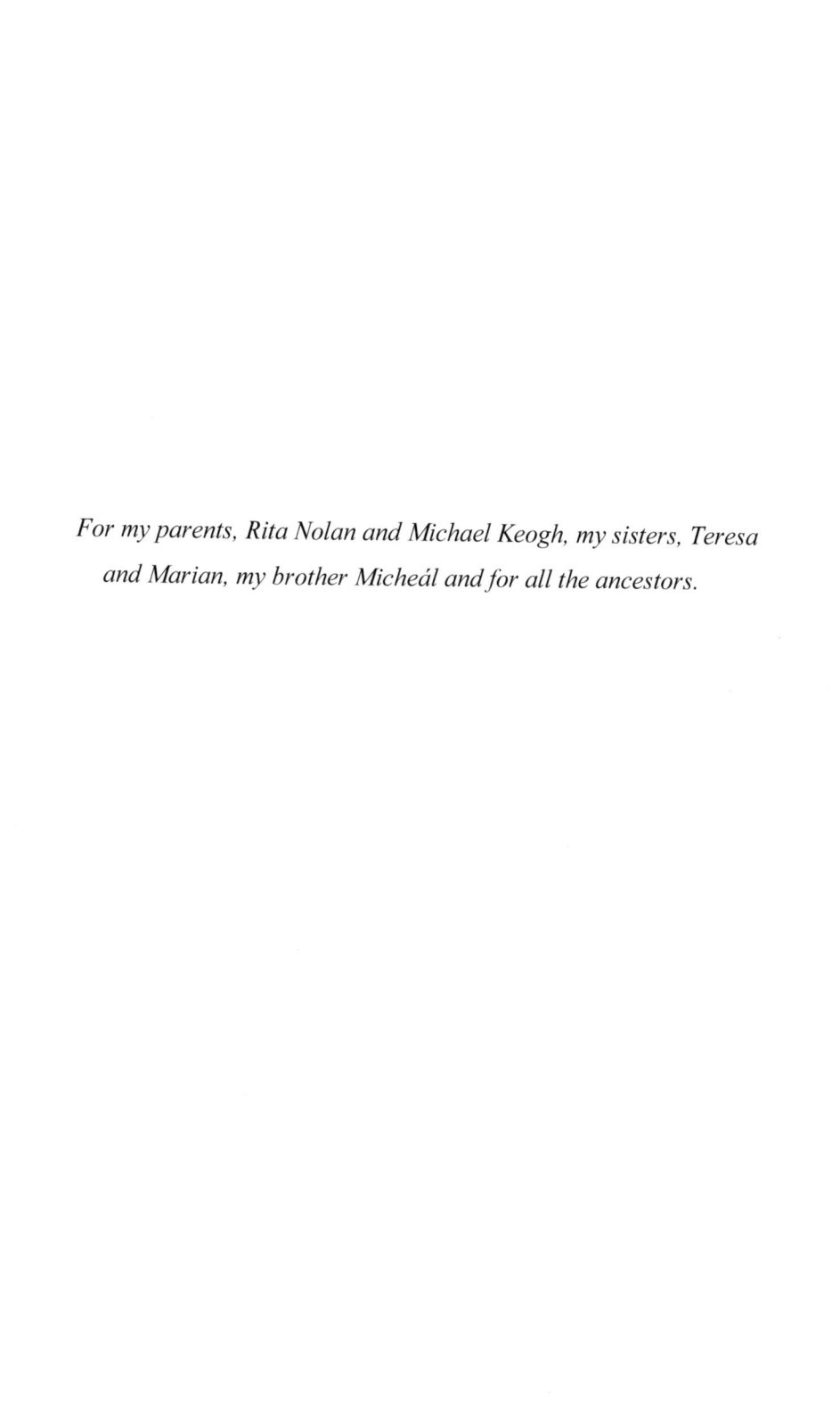

For my parents, Rita Nolan and Michael Keogh, my sisters, Teresa and Marian, my brother Micheál and for all the ancestors.

Author's Note

The Winter Dress is a work of fiction. In writing it, I have drawn on sources rooted in folklore, history, archaeology and language.

Tristledermot, where some of the story is set, is the medieval name for the present-day village of Castledermot, Co Kildare. In medieval times, French, English and Irish were the spoken languages in the town. The majority of those living within the walls were Anglo-Norman, Norman and Saxon.

Rose (Roisín) O'Byrne is referred to as a wild Irish woman. The term the wild Irish refers to the native people who lived outside the town walls.

Rose mentions the images that are carved on the high crosses in Tristledermot. Two of these crosses can still be seen in the grounds of the church of St James.

The Crouched Friars (Fratres Cruciferi), the order to which Brother John belonged, were hospitallers who tended to the sick and those suffering from leprosy. The remains of the leper hospital still stand at St John's in Castledermot.

The novel opens in the grounds of the monastery in Wells, Co Carlow (Irish name *Uilis*). Wells is half-way between Carlow and Kilkenny, near the village of Royal Oak. The ruins of the monastery still stand in the small graveyard there.

Some of the phrases used by Rose are taken from the Irish. For example *Life is a strange son* is a translation of *Is ait an mac an saol* (Literal translation: *It's strange the son of life is*). The Irish word *cumal* is used here to describe a female who is unfree – a slave.

The terms the *good people* and the *Sídhe* refer to the faeries. *A finished musician* is translated from the Irish *ceoltóir críochnaithe*.

The first outbreak of the Black Death in Kilkenny did occur on Christmas Day 1348 and is noted in the diaries of John Clynn.

Chapter 1

Rose

Wells, Ireland, 1348

Winter is no time to travel. The mud of the drenched track has seeped through my shoes and my feet are like ice. The grey sky has long since darkened into night. Ahead, a fire is burning near the monastery in Wells, a place well known for the shelter provided by the monks. It's a welcome distraction from the horror I've left behind. People look me over as I approach – nervous and afraid at first – but then they shift up along the low wooden form to make room for me near the fire.

'God bless us all,' a woman says. I avoid her gaze, not wanting to be caught in conversation. The flames are high and those gathered glow in the light. A strange sensation causes me to see all of the faces as if they are those of my ancestors, of my people from all the vanished years. I see my grandparents and their brothers and sisters, and others with similar features alongside them. I stare deeper into the flames, to try to see only the orange tongues and sparks rising. My mother appears and then my husband; it's more than I can bear and I leave the fireside and move to the small hut near the monastery gate.

The hut is empty, the better place to sit is near the fire. The quietness is a balm after the fireside noise and sights. I feel safe, sure that no one else would welcome the dark, cold stone as I do, but then a lantern

Rose

shows the face of a monk as he bends below the lintel and enters, his frame filling the doorway. His breathing is laboured as if he too has walked a great distance. He holds out his lantern and looks about the hut: the floor rushes are old but dry; the walls are covered in spider webs, and bats roosting in the rafters flit in and out through the open door. My feet are colder than I can ever remember. I try to find a place where the floor rushes are thick to make a mat between me and the cold stone beneath. If a rat or mouse were to satisfy its hunger with a piece of my flesh, I'm not sure I'd feel it.

'It's a cold night,' I call out to the monk, more to mark my presence than to make pleasantries. 'Too cold for the wolves tonight.' He scowls in the low light, I'm unwelcome. He shuffles, sighs wearily, draws a wooden stool up to sit upon and places his lamp on the deep sill. The room is lit now and unoccupied, save for ourselves and the unseen scuttling creatures.

'Would you not do what the others are doing and sit close to the fire?' he says.

He's an ox of a man and, as he waits for my response, the scowl leaves his face and I recognise him. He used to accompany the priest from the Priory, to my clan, every spring and autumn, without fail, to baptise the new babies. They only repeated what old Áine, the midwife, did at each birth but they were always welcomed by my family. I was but a child when last he saw me.

I don't tell him that I can't return to the large crowd. The promise of the company of this monk might provide some small comfort on a frosty

1348

dark night. I want the night to pass without questions, without reliving what has happened. I want to go back to a time before all that. A time when I was a girl, and life was ahead of me like the hope of a warm summer. Back to the time when I first met this monk; when the simple, joyous life beyond the walls of the town was all I had known. I want the gentleness of the light and the room to soothe my tired soul, just for tonight. Then I can start again.

'I don't want to sit too close to a crowd of strangers tonight,' I say.

He ignores my words. He is drawing things out from his satchel and placing them on the shelf. He looks at me but doesn't recognise me. He is clearly uneasy in my company, fidgeting, sighing and then silent.

I take my bone-flute from beneath my damp cloak and begin to play. It's a tune that my father taught me. A slow air. I hear another flute playing along with me, as I often do. I know it's my father's. I'd know his music anywhere. For a moment I'm lost in the melody and familiar notes underneath it. A cough brings me back to the hut and the cold night.

'I have things to do that require some quiet.'

'Music is quieter than silence, sir.'

'Not that screeching, you'll wake the dead.'

Echoes of the other piper hang in the shadows. This music from beyond the grave has never frightened me. My mother always said there was more to be feared from the living than from the dead. In all the years since my father's death, I've met but one other person who could hear that secret music.

Rose

I watch the monk remove implements from a small leather pouch. A little jar, vellum, the tools of a scribe. He stoops into the light, dips something in the jar and begins to write. Although I have often met monks and holy people, I have never seen a scribe at work. Despite his gruff humour, curiosity draws me closer to him. Dark shapes appear on the vellum as he scratches across it.

'Have you no one travelling with you? No husband?' he asks, looking up from his work.

'None.'

His tone is sharp and, seeing my interest in his shape-making, he covers the work to hinder my gaze. He has no need to bother, I cannot read. What I most want is for him to recognise me. Is there anything left of the girl I once was? I want him to remember with me those better days when we were both so much younger.

In the lamp light, his face shows the strong lines of years.

'But I have been married. Four times,' I say quietly.

'Only four?' he asks without meeting my eyes.

'The first man was from just beyond the walls of Tristledermot.'

He stops his work and looks up at me then.

'Have I met you before?'

The devilment in me can't resist teasing him for a moment and not answering him directly.

'I suppose you are on your way to St Moling's holy well? I haven't heard of such crowds travelling this way since I was girl.'

'All of them going there in the hope of being made well,' he snorts.

1348

'You don't believe that the blessed water will cure them?'

'I do not. I've seen a hundred times more cures than you've had husbands and each one was as useless as the last.'

I pretend to misunderstand his words.

'I wouldn't say that; the first one was a good worker, despite his weak leg.'

With that the monk looks more closely at me, his mouth widening into a smile and then he points.

'I do know you, I have met you before. Bless us all, it was many years ago.'

I laugh. His face now has a light of its own. He hesitates again, trying to remember my name, although it's changed since then.

'Rose,' I say and bow to him.

'Rose?'

He's perplexed at the sound of the word. It's not a name used by the wild Irish people. I took the name after I moved to the town.

'Roisín O'Byrne. Rose. The dressmaker's daughter,' I say.

'Roisín, Rose, indeed I know you now.'

He was kind in his youth, and when it was time to marry, it was to the Priory that my husband insisted on going.

'I was married to the man with the weak leg by your lot; they didn't make a great job of it, the marriage didn't last long.'

Something changes then, his face grows dark. Outside I can hear a man praying until another tells him to be quiet, and then a scuffle breaks out. It ends quickly with a roar from a woman who says she has enough

Rose

to do without having to box the ears off grown men.

'Let them that wants to, pray, and let them as has no need for prayers behave in such a manner as to prove it,' she snaps.

The ordinary drone of low conversations returns. The monk begins again to work, his shoulders are hunched and his head is down, paying close attention to his marks.

'Is it from Tristledermot you're coming?' he asks.

'It is.'

'Tell me, are things as bad there as they say?'

He stops his work, waiting for me to talk. It's the question everyone will want an answer to and, if I tell the truth, I could find myself thrown into gaol or carted back home.

'Aren't your lot there? Don't they speak?'

He grunts and continues with his efforts. He moves this way and that, no doubt the ache in his shoulders is a familiar one. I watch the small strokes he makes.

'What are you writing?'

'Words, Rose, words.'

He is irritable. Being a mother is a miraculous occurrence to one who has no child and writing and reading are the same to one who can do neither. The sky through the little gap in the wall is full of stars; there'll be a hard frost tonight. My body shivers, the pit of my stomach is frozen. Don't ignore me, sir, not now, not tonight.

'It's like milking a bull with you; I suppose writing is a way of speaking without saying anything.'

1348

He sighs and turns to me, puts his vellum on his lap and straightens up. The corner of his mouth is trying not to smile.

'I'd have said it was a way of remembering, Rose.'

'Indeed! Some people are gifted in that respect, they can remember every little thing. Every birth, every name, every death. If you are fortunate you'll have someone like that in your family. They hold the memories of everyone else.'

He laughs, reddening as he does.

'That's not always a blessing, Rose. There are plenty who are happier to forget about what's gone on in their family. Plenty would prefer if no one could tell their story.'

No one to tell the story of a family. No trace of the struggles, of the dead children, the years of plenty and the lean years, the kindnesses, the petty mistakes of meanness. Nothing left but bones crumbling beneath the ground.

I think of my cousin Bríon and his lengthy songs. Every time there was a birth in the family he'd add another verse. We all had our own verses and, even though he would spend a whole evening singing a single song and hadn't the best voice, we'd wait for our own part of the ballad and clap or blush along with him. The children, whose memories were still empty, would pick up the words and sing them after he'd gone. Bríon was one of the greatest storytellers I've ever known.

'How do we remember the ones who went before us, without the storytellers? How do we keep a record of the ones who passed the fire back to the sun, for the ones who came afterwards?'

Rose

He looks at me again with disdain on his face.

'You don't really believe that old nonsense, do you?'

I shrug. I don't know what I believe anymore and the ways of the monk are not my ways. Usually I wouldn't bother talking to a religious man about these things; they have narrow views and can't see beyond their noses.

'When we honour the sun, we honour our fathers.'

He snorts again, these things are ridiculous to him.

'And what about our mothers?' He's mocking me, but I ignore him.

'It's the moon that honours our mothers. For a man of words, there's a lot you don't know.'

Putting his vellum beside the satchel on the sill, he stands, his head almost touching the beam overhead. He twirls around, his movements light, graceful and incredibly funny.

'Take a good look at me, Rose, front and back. Do I look like a pagan to you?'

I copy him, twirling. The shadows on the walls make it appear that people are dancing in this small hut.

'And tell me, sir, do I look like a bride to you?'

He places his hands on his hips and laughs now himself.

'You're going again? A fifth time? All I can say is, God bless your energy! And tell me, what happened to the rest of them?'

Chapter 2

Rose

The Clan of the O'Byrnes, Kildare, 1319

My mother was well known for what she could do with cloth. Her bridal dresses were renowned throughout the land. When a family ordered a dress from her, it was known that they respected the bride. My mother made bridal dresses in three layers – wool, linen and cotton. She said that the wearer would never be cold and would have a dress for every season.

If my mother could describe a fastener, a simple man of the family, Milo, could make it. Milo could make fasteners from anything. Bones, pebbles, clay and what he couldn't do with a carving knife wasn't worth doing. He could carve the likeness of any animal into wood, and even the face of a person, if the mood came on him. My mother would cover the fasteners or buttons that Milo made with fabric. The effect was one of indulgence and beauty. People often came to a wedding just to see the bridal dress.

Tomás O'Toole came to our dwelling to order a dress for his sister, their father being dead and their mother being in poor health. It was the way he asked for the thing that got my attention.

'My sister is planning to marry and I want her husband and his

Rose

family to know what a treasure they are to be blessed with.'

He placed a pouch of coins on the table, more coin than we had ever seen in one transaction. He had reared and sold a full batch of hens, half a dozen young boars, and as many pigeons, squirrels and ducks as he could catch, in order to raise the money for his sister's dress.

His words caused me to study his face. I don't believe I ever saw more handsome eyes. Dark and misty like the river in the morning. My mother smiled, she always liked to see women well thought of. They talked about the particulars and before he left he waved at me. I smiled too and returned his salute; only when he was walking away did I remember his limp.

My mother took up her work again and turned to me.

'There are some things even more important than two straight legs,' and we laughed because joy recognises joy.

The dress took three months to make. My mother herself went to the town to order the fabric from a merchant there. The merchant, Hugh Darcy, had very little cloth in his store, a recent load of goods had been stolen by thieves along the road to Moone. My mother liked Hugh and found him honest, so she waited for his next delivery, which arrived a week later, and we started the work in earnest. We made as fine a gown as we were capable of making, a dress fit for a queen. It was as green as the leaves of a spring chestnut and the trims were made from linen with flecks of gold. Each button on the outer layer was embroidered and the inner ones were fastened with clasps of small carvings of animals, crosses, berries, the symbols of fertility, of spring, of safety. Tomás

1319

came often to watch us work and we talked and he joked. I looked forward to his visits. Talk of a wedding makes talk of another, they say. This was true for me. Tomás had a way about him that lifted my spirits always.

When he asked me to marry him I had no answer but yes. I was fifteen and one of the oldest unmarried women in the clan. My mother said I should start my own work in Tomás's dwelling but I couldn't leave her to do all the work herself. And so I told Tomás that I would work with my mother by day but I would come to him by night and he agreed to this.

In the weeks before marriage, we walked in the evenings, just to be alone. The light was in the sky until late and the hills we lived in faced west. If we heard a traveller coming towards us we would hide until they passed. You could never be too careful in those troubled times.

It was a red evening and we were on our home journey when we heard voices and the clanking of weapons. We ran for the cover of the boulders and the furze and lay still as the soldiers passed. There was always a fear that they would push us from our homes again. They continued on and as we stood, I saw Tomás's face change, and then his body, and I saw him as a boy. I saw his father, too, and his mother as a young woman, and they were light and full with happiness. 'Roisín, Roisín,' Tomás was calling me, and then he changed again into the man I knew and the vision was over.

I didn't say a word to Tomás but I hurried home to tell my mother about it. As I spoke she grew paler and warned me not to tell a soul. 'They'll call you witch,' she said.

Tomás wanted a religious wedding and I would have done anything to please him. We travelled to Tristledermot to the Priory, were married and were told our names were to be written in the book. Several of the young monks attended the wedding and sang beautiful hymns. It was the church marriage that Tomás wanted. The wedding was in Latin and we had no idea what was said but we said our own words to each other and felt the profounder things that are beyond what a word can mean. When it was all done and finished, we turned home to our own traditional celebration with our two families.

A full summer and autumn I lived between my mother and Tomás. I took on more of my mother's work and, because we were happy, people liked to come to us. There was plenty of food that year, for a change, and I looked out at the future with great hope. Tomás concerned himself with the care of his mother and she was content with his efforts. At night I loved to lie next to my husband, listening to the sounds of the house settle and feeling the warmth of him against me and inside me. His touch was tender and loving and safe. He stirred feelings in me that were beyond anything I had ever imagined, and all the while my love grew deeper and deeper.

Winter came hard that year. Tomás was struck down with an affliction of the chest and within a month he was in bed and I was tending to him, as well as to his mother. He was as sweet and uncomplaining a man as I

1319

have ever met, even on his death bed. The morning before his spirit took flight, despite his shallow breath, he sat in the small bed, took my hand and looked on me with such love that even without the words I knew how much he adored me.

Leaving this world is never easy, not for the old or the young, but Tomás never said any word that wasn't good. 'I'm so blessed,' he would say as I washed his brow, 'to think that I married you.'

I loved his soft kisses against the back of my hands, and the memories of the nights we spent warm together were never far from me when I was near him. The healer visited and administered poultices for his fever and she showed me how to bind his chest and keep him warm with hot stones in his bed.

Tomás's sister visited often. She was full with the promise of a child. Sorrow can make carrying difficult; a baby can draw itself into the world too soon with the weight of sadness pulling on it. Tomás was always cheerful when he saw her, asking about her husband, remembering the happiness at her wedding. I learned as much about life from his dying as I had from his living.

'You'll marry again, my love,' he said one day. 'I can't bear to think of you lonely'.

I told him that no man could be his match. He insisted that his sister would help me find a good man. 'Not too religious, or he'll bend you in half. Someone who can provide for you and let you work as you wish. Your gowns are things of beauty; you must keep making them.'

Rose

Before Tomás fell ill, I had been making him a new tunic. My mother said that he must be very vain to want such a thing but Tomás knew nothing of the tunic. I stitched a trim onto it, like I had for his sister's dress, except I put the images from the high crosses at Tristledermot on it. Bible scenes wound their way around the cloth. Daniel and the lions and the loaves and fishes and the cross of Saint Brighid. There's some would complain about that, but there's always some who enjoy complaining about the work of others.

It was hard to find time in daylight to complete it. One night, when I found the opportunity, I called to my mother and she presented me with the finished garment. She had completed it. 'What he can't wear in life he may as well wear in death,' she said and we wept together and held each other for a long time.

Despite the arguments with the religious men, and the occupation by the strangers of the valley, we still had our own burial ground on the hill above Tristledermot. It was sometimes beyond the strength or will of a family to carry a body to it, and the cold arms of winter made it twice as long a walk. The graveyard the monks wanted us to use was on cursed ground and no one wanted to bury anyone there. The foreigners had taken the very land of our burial ground and it was a risk to return. Some of the men went ahead of us to dig. On a lonely day in winter, my sister, my mother and I followed Tomás's broken body to the hill. Although I was heavy-hearted with grief, the kind words and small deeds that Tomás had done filled my mind and gave me the strength to stagger in the wind to his final resting place.

1319

I cared for Tomás's mother as best I could but without her son she faded fast and joined him before the week was out. A home is a steady place to heal but I had a restlessness in me. Tomás's sister gave birth to a little girl and, although I felt happiness for her, I was sick with jealousy. My mother kept telling me that things would change again and this sadness in me would leave, but I didn't believe her. People told me that he was with God, and maybe he was, but I didn't have faith in their words. I liked to think of him as the light of the morning and the earth under my feet. I felt as if he were holding my every step.

Tomás was as holy a man as I'd ever known. Not one demand did he place on me or upon his family but rather lived to see them contented. He kept Lent and tried to keep up with the rules of the church, but he never expected me to go along with him. There are more rules in the church than a woman like me could follow, and in any case the O'Byrnes still lived by the old ways. It seems to me that the church wanted rid of the traditions and laws we have.

Tomás told me of a law that says only the first marriage of a person is counted and only if it's done by a priest. They call any other children, outside of that first marriage, *whoreson*, with no rights to as much as the name of their father.

Everything they do is in favour of the men, although I know many men are not happy with this new law. They want to take away the power of a person to leave a marriage. We had our own ways of managing ourselves and didn't need anyone else to do it for us.

I prayed for Tomás when he was sick, I offered flowers to the saints

Rose

and went on a pilgrimage to the holy well at Tristledermot, for all the good it did. I'm not the first young widow and I won't be the last.

'You are lucky you were born an O'Byrne,' my mother reminded me and, despite my grief, I knew she was right. It's peculiar how much you can miss someone whom you've known just a short while. Before Tomás arrived in my life, there was no gap in me but, after he died, there was an empty land stretching as far as I could see.

Tomás had told me to stay in the dwelling after him, but I couldn't stay there without him and I went back home to my mother. Conn and the elders of the clan ruled that I should give the place to Tomás's sister's family and I was happy with their judgement.

I wore heavy clothes all that month, and even covered my head. It was hot but the more uncomfortable I was, the closer I felt to Tomás. At night I thought I could hear him calling me and I called out to him, wishing with all my heart that my voice would lift the veil between this world and the next. My mother took me to be blessed in the Priory in Tristledermot and two things happened. The nightmares stopped and, on the way home, I met my future husband.

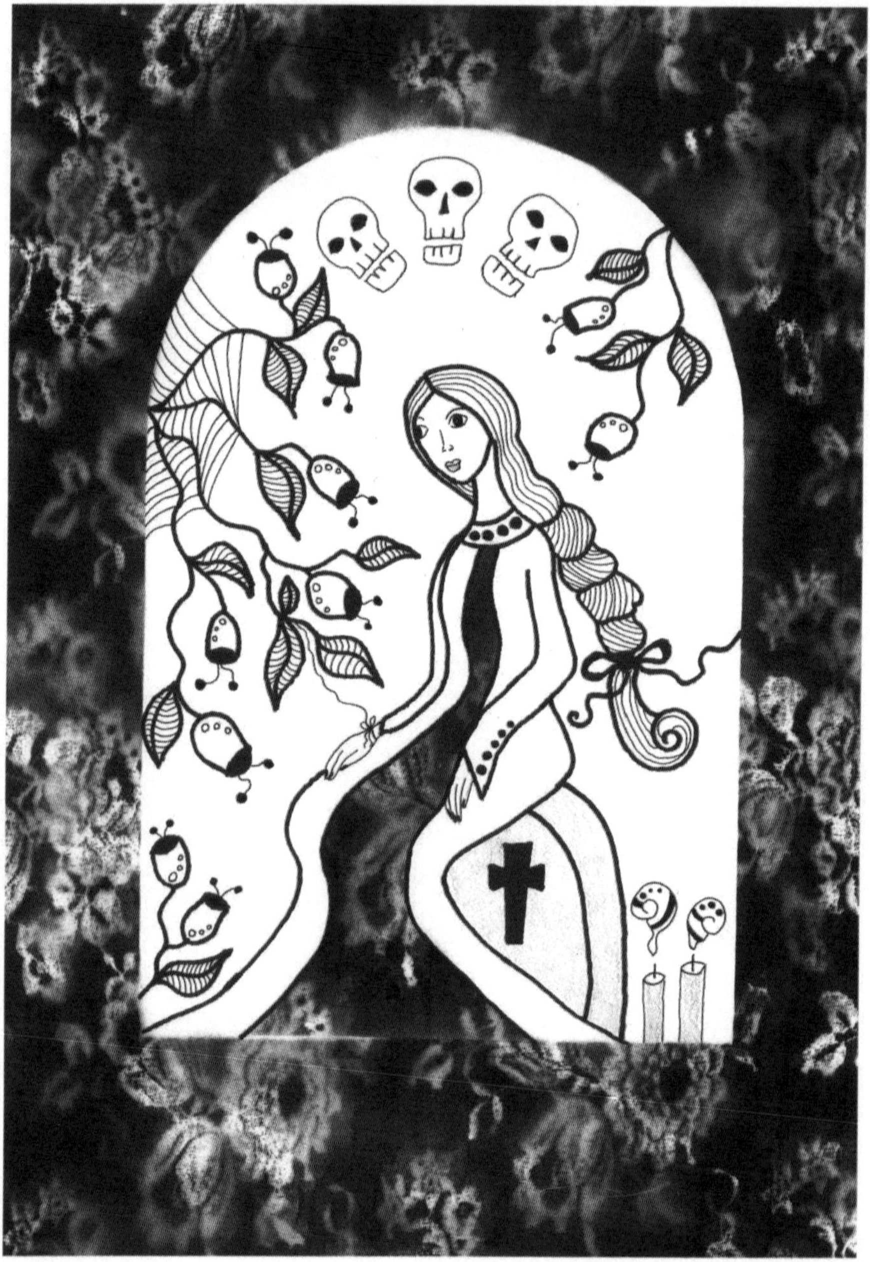

Chapter 3
Rose
Wells, Ireland, 1348

'What made your husband lame?'

The monk's words break through my thoughts and dreaming and I return to the cold night in the dim hut.

I explain to the Monk. 'Tomás won that limp in a battle against the foreigners. There's a wood near our clan that has provided shelter for us as long as we have lived there; fuel for our hearths, willow for the fencing of animals and timber for the building of our dwellings. Tomás was felling a tree that was to hold up the roof of his new home, when the foreigners attacked him and the others who were with him. His cousin was killed and Tomás's leg was injured. The wound healed but the limp was set after that. My darling Tomás was dead within a year of our wedding.'

The monk's face is kindly. I wish we had a small fire to warm us. Plenty have died from the cold on a night like this one.

'It was too short a life. So many lives are too short.'

My talk of Tomás causes him to remember something.

'That Priory, where you married, was home to me from the age of seven.'

'You must be a saint by now.' I laugh.

He is sharpening a small wooden implement. The vellum now has many words written on it.

'What are you about?'

'I'm sharpening this nib. The finer the point, the finer the letters.'

'I expect it was the monks who taught you this?'

'They did not. My mother taught me how to read and write long before I met the monks.'

A woman who can read among my people is a rare thing. This monk has come from a family with wealth. Who else but the wealthy and the religious people have the time to learn such things?

'What does it say, sir?'

'It says *She moved across the purple night, her face, her legs in candlelight.*'

I observe his features closely. He seems to be in earnest and yet I'm bewildered by what he has said. It's not what I had expected.

'Your own mother taught you this?'

His temper rises, as if I have offended his craftsmanship.

'No, Rose. My mother taught me *how* to write, these words are my own. From my own head.'

I suppose it's no different from the songs of Bríon, those words came from his own head.

'I was hoping for something biblical. A story to shorten this perishing night.'

'Did you think I was writing a bible story? Are you conversant with the Latin tongue?'

He's teasing me again now. These religious men look down on us.

1348

As if a person who can't read has no mind of worth.

'Yes, I speak the Latin very well. All my people do.'

'You? You can speak Latin?'

'Yes, very well. Through my arse.'

The sound of our laughter fills the night.

The monk has taken to me now. His work has stopped and his shoulders are straight again. He makes a bargain with me. We will tell a single story each and then I'm to leave him in peace to get on with his business. I'm relieved that he doesn't mention sleep. His own thoughts are perhaps as troubled as mine. He insists that I begin. I wait for a story to come to me. That's the way with tales, even the old ones. They seem to come out of the earth and take time to settle themselves fully.

'In the place beyond the walls, where I come from, there's a tale about a woman called Oonagh.'

I think about my cousin Bríon and his brother, who liked to tell this story and how they would name every one of their neighbours when they told it. And then they would fabricate conversations and exchanges that might have fallen between them.

'Unlike your own kinswomen from the town, *we* are free to travel alone. One evening Oonagh was returning from a neighbouring family where she had been trading. On her return journey the darkness had crept in early and the shapes ahead were making all kinds of creatures in the dusk. She was afraid, as anyone might be, of stray soldiers but not as afraid as she was of the Sídhe who might gather around her. Then she heard a wailing and sobbing through the darkness, and even though she wanted to turn and run, and even though she thought it might be a trick, the voice was so pitiful she couldn't ignore it. She thought of her own children and how she hoped others might help them if they were ever in a bind.

"'I'm coming," she said. And her heart was pounding in her chest as she walked into the dark.

'She found a young man lying on the ground, tied up and yelping and whining like a pup. She unsheathed her knife, cut the rope, hauled the man up and brought him home. The man slept like a corpse for seven days and seven nights and on the eighth day he woke, healed of his wounds. Oonagh made a lover out of the young man. And the sounds of love-making that were heard coming from her dwelling – people are still talking about them today!'

When my cousin Bríon and his brother told it, they used to wail and thrash each other with passionate embraces, worse than animals, and if there were newly married people in the family they would cry out their names until someone called stop.

'Her family were afraid of the young man, because he never spoke a word, had the strength of ten men and never tired from work. And when the moon came full he would get restless, like all those who are close to the underworld. He stayed through the winter and when the spring moon came full, he disappeared. Oonagh went out of her mind with the want of him. Her appearance changed for the worse. She begged her people to help her find him but they laughed and offered her the loan of a bull to help with her particular trouble. She took to wandering the countryside

1348

searching for him, and they say that in her madness she lay with a he-wolf. The offspring of this union grew in number and took to wandering among us. You could be beside one right now and have no knowledge of it. They have the body of a person and the cruel savagery of a wolf.'

I stand closer to the monk and make the shadow shape of a beast and growl. The monk laughs at my efforts to frighten him. It's not something at which I was ever accomplished. Brion would have told the tale so much better.

'A wounded heart is a lonely hunter indeed, Rose,' the monk says eventually.

'But the peculiar thing is, sir, not a wolf was seen in the area again after that.'

'Those were the days when wolves were the greatest danger we knew.'

I know before he opens his mouth what his next question will be.

'Is it as bad, Rose, in Tristledermot as they say?'

Even though I don't want to talk about it, the truth spills from me.

'I remember the year that the cattle fell dead where they stood. And I remember the old people talking about the time that there was no food to be had in the country. I've heard the stories from the old people and remember the destruction and injury that was done by the Bruces, but in all the years that I have lived, nothing could have prepared me for the occurrences in Tristledermot since the nights lengthened this autumn. I know you are talking of the pestilence, sir, I have never seen anything like it. Have you?'

Rose

The monk settles himself again and stares into the lamp light.

'The first time I encountered the pestilence was in a port town in France. When I arrived in the port, it was one of the busiest places I have ever seen. Ships coming and going, markets everywhere, people buying and selling, people coming from all over the world. A week after I reached the place, the pestilence arrived. A week later, the only sounds that could be heard were the screaming of the dying, and the wailing of families as they buried their dead. I cleared out of the town shortly after that.'

How my mother would have loved to hear about the markets of which the monk speaks. She loved to hear the merchants describe the ports of Dublin, New Ross or Waterford. Endless goods being loaded onto the ships for trading abroad, as far south, they said, as Persia and all kinds of goods coming from places unheard of. Rolls of cloth of every texture and colour were loaded onto carts to go to the cloth markets where they would be bought by merchants and taken to other towns.

The monk's account of the arrival of the pestilence resembles the horror of our own town. The cruel shock we got when we realised what threatened us, and the cold terror of each family, was almost as bad as the disease itself. We suffered unspeakable fear while we waited for the verdict of Fate and more horror beyond that when the pestilence slunk into our houses.

'Tell me, sir, did they ever find a cure that helped?' I ask the monk.

'They did not. Not at all, although there were people who claimed to

1348

have. I was in the town of Bristowe when the pestilence broke out there. There was an apothecary in the town who had a poultice of herbs which he'd put on the boils and even on the open sores. But then the people discovered that the herbs were mixed with human excrement. No wonder people died screaming in agony.'

People in Tristledermot spoke of many cures. All were tried and all failed. There was a rumour that a cure was to be had abroad in Rome. I am strangely comforted by the monk's words. There is no cure for the pestilence, not here, not abroad. A doubt that had being gnawing at the back of my mind finally stops. Although there's another doubt living in me, a question that I'm afraid to ask and yet I must.

'What causes it? Do you think it's a punishment from God?'

The monk sweeps his hand downwards through the air, dismissively.

'I do not! I used to think it was carried by the wind or some corruption of the air, but sometimes the wind would come from the east, and another time the wind would come from the west and still the pestilence came, so I realised that it couldn't be the wind. I met a man in a French town who swore to me it was carried by women. "You can blame women for a lot of things," I said, "but you can't blame them for that." More said it was the Jews that brought it but there was no substance in that kind of talk. I've seen men who mind themselves, men who eat the finest of food, with servants seeing to their every need and they get it, and I've seen men who are dragging the corpses, with hardly enough food to keep body and soul together, and they don't get it. I've seen good men die and the worst of knaves who didn't catch it. The one

Rose

thing I do know is that it seems to travel by night. People go to bed in the whole of their health and wake up covered in the boils and the sores.'

With that the monk falls silent for a time and we both keep to our own thoughts. And then the monk speaks again, softly.

The angel comes in the dark of night,
His cloak is black, his eyes are bright,
He looks upon the sick and well,
But which is which, not one can tell.

The old people say that when the heart breaks suddenly, the memory breaks too. Perhaps I will have the blessing of a broken memory.

'I began to imagine an avenging angel on every corner and I couldn't stop thinking of it, and of the story from the Old Testament. People would put a mark on their doors at night and any door that didn't have a mark, the angel would come and take the first born – it could be a dog or a cat or a child, but by morning the first born in the house would be dead.'

'They've been putting marks on all the doors in Tristledermot,' I say. 'All the doors are now marked with the sign of the cross. I expect that's why they are doing it.'

'For all the good it'll do them, it'll do them no good at all,' he says.

A donkey startles us both with its braying, a lengthy declaration to the night. Everyone is afraid of the pestilence, it's worse than anything they can imagine. I hear the town gates of most places are locked. Even so I'm hopeful that I'll get in to Kilkenny. This monk must be soft of

1348

head to go back to a place that is so full of death. Perhaps his faith protects him.

'There were omens, you know. Signs that this was coming.'

'Omens?' he asks.

'In the spring of this year, the baker's wife cut bread and blood spilled from the centre of it, on three Sundays after the feast of St Valentine. And beyond the walls, this summer gone, birds were said to have deserted their nests.'

If he doesn't believe me he shows no sign of it. And then he says that he saw that same omen, the blood drawn from bread, painted on the wall of a church in France and that he heard it in England too.

A chill rises up my spine. What hope is there if the same fate is coming to each land?

'It could be the end of all things,' I say.

The monk discards this idea with another wave of his hand.

'Sure any day could be the end. What does it say in the Bible? *We know not the day nor the hour.*'

For the months before it came, we'd heard about the pestilence and were under the weight of the worry of it. And then the first sign of it in a man from the town by the name of Scroope was talked about, but we couldn't be sure even after he died.

The monk is humming a foreign tune and then says:

There once was a lassie called Rose,

Who was skilled in the making of clothes

A dress, or a shroud, of which you'd be proud,

But you'd also be dead, I suppose.

We both laugh heartily, he has the gift of laughter and I am grateful to him for sharing it with me this night. I tell him that the lines are such that his mother would be proud, that he had put to good use all the words she had taught him.

'You never know, she might hear it herself soon enough,' I say.

'Thank you! Do I look that bad? Do I appear to be at death's door myself?'

I tease him then and repeat back to him his own words about none of us knowing the day nor the hour assigned to our death. His laughter fades into silence again and he stares into the lamp, as if looking for something within it.

'Is that why you returned, sir, are you running from the pestilence?'

He shifts his position, stretches out and gives up the search in the light. The length of his body and width of his arms are almost the length and breadth of the room.

'Running from the pestilence, Rose, and now it seems I'm running towards it. Many years ago, I set out to travel east, with the intention of visiting the birthplace of Jesus. When I was in Bristowe, England, I fell in with a group of Pilgrim Knights who said they had the same intention but, by the time we got to France, I realised that their only interest in travelling east was to kill people and take that which did not belong to them. So I spent years wandering about Europe and back up to England and Bristowe and here I am, after all this time, on my way back to Tristledermot, never having visited the birthplace of Christ.'

1348

He looks like a man who has lost something of great importance, without which he is not complete. Something that compelled him to wander the world in search of it; I wonder if it is his faith or his family. Are there any of us left who haven't lost either one or the other or both? A sudden faintness creeps over me, the lamp grows bright. It's a familiar feeling although it hasn't happened for many years now. I can't be sure if it's happening in my head or in the room but a vision appears before me.

Age rolls away from the face of the monk, his skin smooths and his hair becomes a scraggy mane of light. He is a boy again. Beside him stands another boy, a little taller but with the same fair hair and the bluest eyes. They take off, running into a stream. Water catches the sunlight as they splash through it, laughing, and then someone screams from a distance and before the boys can even turn to find out what's happening, a warrior on horseback snatches one of them. The warrior scoops him onto the horse, carrying him like a sack of meal. The boy on the ground looks on as the rider and the boy disappear through a high but open wooden gateway.

'What's the matter, Rose? Are you ill?'

All of the light folds back into the darkness of the night, to where I am, but the image stays with me of the haunted face of the boy who was left behind, and the terror of the boy who was carried away.

Chapter 4
Brother John
Wells, 1348

Rose blesses herself and mutters prayers in her own tongue. She is pale and breathing fast, as if she has been running. Her eyes in the lamplight are half closed; it's as if she is sleepwalking. I wait for her to awaken, it's well known that a disturbance for a person, who is in this state, can be injurious.

Her questions have induced melancholy and warmth in me. All these years I have been longing to return home, knowing that home, as I knew it, is gone now, but longing for some remaining shred of a different place and time all the same. I've felt like an outsider all of my life. The dressmaker's talk is comforting, not because of her stories or her sad account of things in the town, but because of the way she speaks to me, as if she and I are from the same place, as if she and I belong there.

She stirs again and begins to awaken. Her hair and the red glow of the lamp are of one colour. She speaks but in her own tongue and I can't understand her. I ask her gently what she is trying to say.

'He was taken, wasn't he? By men on horseback.'

'Who?'

'The child whose hair was fair and whose eyes were as blue as the midsummer sky. A boy who was in the same body as yourself. A twin. You were playing in the river near your home when he was taken away through a great open gateway. I heard a woman scream his name, Alvery, and I heard him call your name, Fabien.'

She is sincere in her speech. I've lived long enough to have seen many devils at work and a league of rogues engaged in trickery. I've seen just two whose visions were pure beyond question – this woman and the old crusader I met when I was a boy at the monastery. She makes the sign of the cross and prays again in her own tongue and then says:

'May his sweet and innocent soul be always at the right-hand side of God. I'm so very sorry, sir, for your loss.'

I can hear yet again the cries of my brother as he was torn away from me, and the echoes of my mother's screams are again all around me. I've prayed since that time for the grace to forgive and to understand the will of God, yet I have never received these gifts. Anger rises up in me, as it always does when I think of that day. Anger at the bandits, but mostly anger at myself, for not turning to see the men coming and for not being able to call out to my brother or to help him in any way. I remained frozen in the place where I stood until my father came to my aid.

'He was taken by your people, Rose, by the wild Irish. He was six years old. And seven nights after they took him, his body was tossed back over the wall. A small bundle of bloody rags thrown in a heap for my mother to find.'

'There's fierce cruelty on both sides, sir. I am sorry beyond measure for your desperate loss.'

1348

She puts a hand on my shoulder and the anger leaves me. It seems to flow through her body and into the night.

I ask Rose about these visions, how frequently they have occurred and what is the nature of the things they reveal? She tells me that they come at their own will, not often and only with certain people. The first time it happened she was a girl and since then perhaps a dozen have come. There is no evidence of any evil in her account and the peace that her words have brought me can only be divine in nature.

'I told my mother about the visions but she said that I wasn't to speak of them.'

'I'd say your visions are a gift from God, Rose.'

She smiles when I say this and her face is radiant, yet it stirs a deep pity in me. I recognise sorrow in her eyes. I don't ask what has put it there, sadness sometimes has more need of sanctuary than speech. She sighs deeply, rubs her arms against the cold and then turns to me saying, 'This talk of God reminds me of our bargain. A story from each of us, and I have fulfilled my part of it, it's your turn now, sir.'

The last thing I want to do is tell a bible story. All of the years of teaching people, of trying to shine the light of faith, of trying to inspire in them devotion to Jesus and to the Church, and now my own faith is so dim, I'm ashamed to utter the words I once spoke so firmly. I am quiet for some time until I see that she won't relent. The wild Irish never forget a bargain made.

'I will tell you the story of Daniel in the lions' den.'

'Everyone knows that story.'

Brother John

I search my mind for a story that will entertain her, something to satisfy her wish to shorten the night.

'I'll tell you the story of Bathsheba then. Do you know that one?'

She smiles again, she's heard it before but wants to hear it, it's always popular among pagans and people who are not pious. I tease her and tell her it might offend someone of her virtue but if it pleases her, I will take the chance.

'David was a great king of the Israelites. A handsome man. Tall, good-looking, strong, someone who would appeal to a woman like yourself.'

She laughs at my teasing and it pushes me on.

'He drove all the enemies of the Lord before him. His palace walls were plated with gold and silver. One evening, as he's walking on the roof of the palace, he sees a beautiful woman bathing in the river. Her body is naked and she glows like the sun. And his heart is going thump thump thump and other bits of him are going thump thump, too.'

Rose chuckles at this.

'He called one of his servants. "Who is the woman in the water?" he asked. "Oh that's Bathsheba," says the servant, "she's the wife of Uriah – one of your warriors."

'And he stays there watching Bathsheba bathe and determines to meet her.

'The next day he sends for her and, in his chamber, he takes her into bed. But that's not enough for David; he wants to marry her. He orders her husband to be placed in the front line of battle and, within days,

1348

Uriah is killed. The death of her husband causes Bathsheba great agony but, no more than yourself, Rose, she gets over it. She marries David and a child is born to them some months later. But the Lord above is watching all of this and brings His wrath upon the house of David and the infant dies. And that's the story of David and Bathsheba.'

'That's a sad story, sir, and a cruel thing for a God to do.'

She falls silent. This story, that had once seemed so righteous to me, now seems brutal, but it's not only the story that has upset Rose; it's something else, something that is trying to find its way to the surface. I tell her that I've often thought the same thing myself.

'Tell me, Rose, where are you bound for?'

She is as still as the night air and shows no sign of hearing me speak. I don't ask again and instead try to think of a way to break the solemn mood that has settled on her. I stand behind her as I recite a poem, inhaling the smell of wood-smoke from her hair, the smell of the earth itself.

O Rose, who knows how long we'll live,
This might be your last chance to give,
So take off your dress in the dark of the night
For we may be dead by the morning light.

She's a beautiful woman and as entertaining as a male companion. For a moment I forget the poem, lost in her presence, until I hear her ask me what it is I'm doing. She is nervous of my closeness to her, as any woman might be, and steps away. My efforts to entertain did not please her. She points to the parchment and in a sharp tone asks: 'Are those tools not the property of a monastery?' It's not a concern of hers; she is trying to needle me.

For years I worked as a copyist and then as a scribe. The job of the scribe is to write the happenings of our patrons. The births, deaths, marriages and any extraordinary thing that might occur. All in Latin. It has never been a language that gave me the freedom to write as I wish, and the subject matter we had been given was poor. How could we record those details, as if the lives of the wealthy were more impressive than those of the poor? I'm a monk who has taken vows of poverty, shunning the advantages of our clerical brothers who enjoy the status of priests. I have no interest in the lives of the privileged. I'm interested now only in my own work. Something in me longs always to write my own words in my own language. Others are doing it. Her people have been doing it for years. I want to paint with language that which I see and feel. I can't explain the force within that calls me to do it. It is the same force that used to call me to pray.

The Dean once discovered a poem I had written and I was required to wear thorns under my robes for three days. My skin was so cut and blistered that I couldn't lie down for seven nights. I stole from the Priory what tools I needed in order to write, when I could, and I made my own ink and nibs. Unlike the Dean, my mother never deemed it to be the devil's work. Like all things created, there is the highest use and the lowest for it. I have copied the words of others countless times, written the accounts of rascals for years, until my vexation with the bad use of vellum became intolerable. Why can't a plain man be inspired to write

1348

what's in his heart? Jesus Himself wouldn't object to such an act.

I have often wondered how different my life might have been had we stayed in my mother's beloved France. She always lamented our departure, although she had no choice in the matter once the family she was attached to had determined to move. The entire household moved; the promise of wealth and positions were appealing. I believe there were disturbances in the country of France and my mother's bondsmen were assured of a peaceful future in these English lands. I could have told them, even as a boy, that there is nowhere on this earth where men don't fight over land. How is it that men don't behave as tenants of the Lord alone? On my travels the times that were most peaceful were those spent in the silent churches or in the dwellings of the poor. Places where the wicked plunder to their own ends and generate terror amidst the peace. Surely that is the handiwork of Satan.

The sound of rushes moving on the floor brings my attention back to Rose.

'The tools of the scribe, Rose, belong with the scribe.'

I speak gently to her, her face is pale and sad. Perhaps she's better left alone. I sit again and try to gather my thoughts to write. It's hard to see properly in this light, I fear that I will go blind before I can finish my work. If my King had ordained for me a different birth, different nationhood, I might have become a wandering bard and been contented beyond my dreams with that life. The mystery of God's robes is beyond my reason and my lot was with the side of the church. On dark days like this one I'm grateful for that mercy alone. Soldiery would have been an

Brother John

unnatural occupation for one like me.

I had hoped to take on an apprentice. A boy whom I could teach to write, who could transcribe my own words for me. One who could help me as my eyes failed, but my efforts to employ one fell short. I write in the dimness. The ink darkens as it dries and I hold the blotting cloth to the stain of a small blob that has fallen from my quill.

'God in Heaven, how am I to create smooth words in this hovel?'

Christ, I wish I was in the sanctuary of the monastery with my level table and brighter light.

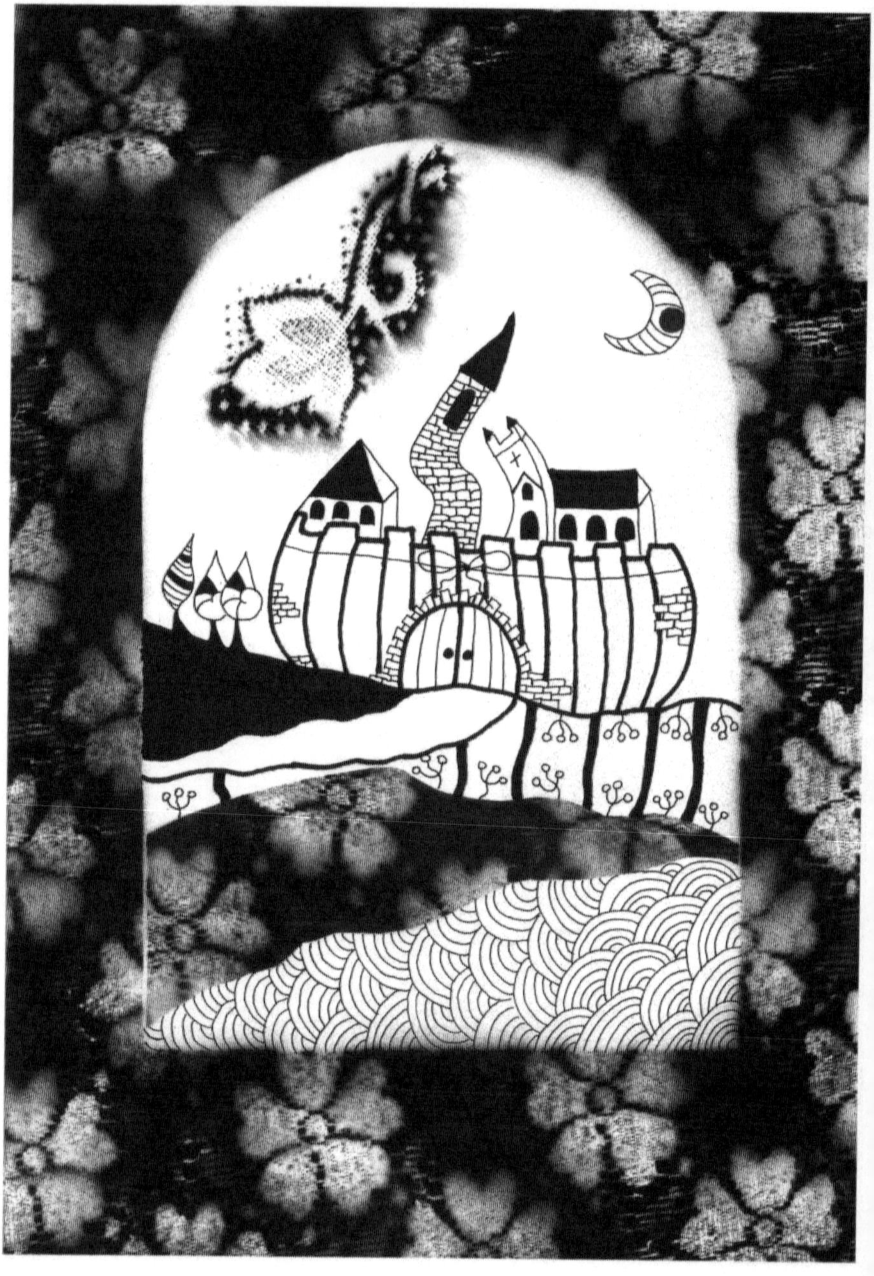

Chapter 5

Rose

Moving to the town of Tristledermot, Kildare, 1319

Against my will I accompanied my mother to the town, on the morning of the first full moon after the death of Tomás. I had no desire to listen to a monk and no faith in their blessings. Although the Priory of Saint John lay outside the walls, my mother wished to enter the town. The passage through the gate was never straightforward. The guards installed there could be villainous with us. If the mood took them towards theft, they could remove some of our goods and charge us the toll for them too. On that day, as it happened, the guards were pleasant; it was market day and they were too busy to detain us. We paid our toll and passed unhindered.

The stench was thick around us. Everywhere there was building happening, the clanging of metal and stone was deafening. There was no end to the numbers of people in the town. Some stared at us directly, we were different to them in our dress and hair. As we made our way to the cloth merchant's dwelling we passed stalls of goods along the road. Outside the butcher's dwelling, a great number of carrion birds were devouring entrails that had been thrown to them. The huge birds blocked our path and we edged our way around them. The butcher, a man with arms like a bull, called out to us and then laughed. I didn't understand him but I smiled. He came towards us and, with a clap of his hands, all the birds took flight. He held his two hands up and then pointed at me and shouted something, clapping again. In my own tongue, I thanked him and passed on.

Jehan Darcy, the son of Hugh, was known well to my mother. He was a handsome giant of a man. The family had traded in yarns and cloths for years. He greeted us and then my mother addressed him.

'I'm sorry for your loss, Jehan, your father was a noble man.'

'He was, Brighid, a man of honour. He said you had the gift of genius with cloth and the gift of honesty with coin.'

'Hugh will be sorely missed. May his soul be seated at the right hand of God,' she said.

He thanked her and told her then that a woman of great standing was looking for a bridal gown.

'Aren't we all of standing?' asked my mother.

'Your work is finer than any I know. This woman is wealthy and will pay you well for the work.'

'We are all of a kind in the eyes of God,' said my mother. 'Your father used to say that to me.'

Yet she agreed to meet the woman. Jehan acted as a translator. And so we entered the house of the foreign woman, a solid house of stone with two fires burning high within. The woman was soft spoken and disarmed my mother with a smile. Jehan spoke the two languages and to start with was locked in what sounded like a dialogue of pleasantries with the foreigner. She showed us the most beautiful cloth and my

1319

mother forgot her bad temper. She presented to us one of her own dresses but shaking her head said this wasn't what she wanted, she wanted a traditional gown, such that we would make for one of our own.

The place was unlike anything I'd ever seen before. In the corner of her room were books. The lady, whose name was Cateline Durant, followed my gaze and moved to a small table upon which was placed an open book. She brought it to me. It wasn't the words upon it I wished to see, I didn't have the letters. It was the patterns and drawings on the pages that were so beautiful. It was as if they sang and my eyes heard the music. I had never met a woman with letters before and this one thing earned my respect more than all her wealth could have done.

My mother spoke to Jehan. 'Our family made clothes for kings of Ireland until the foreigners came. Now the kings are dying and the foreigners have driven us further out. If she wants this dress she can come to our dwelling for fitting, where I have my tools and yarn. I'll not walk the length of the path to fit her.'

My mother is not fond of walking but her response surprised me. It seemed to me that she didn't want the work. My feet were suddenly cold and impatient.

'Then you must stay until it's finished,' Jehan said.

'I must do nothing,' said my mother. 'I'll stay or go as I please. If she wants our work she can come to me. That's my final say. I'll not be a servant to her.'

My mother was a proud woman. She was forced thrice to move from her home. The burning of the old rath when she was a child and the force of the soldiers was not something she could have fought with any hope of success but this order was something she could resist and her refusal was an act of resistance against all the other forced actions.

Cateline turned the pages of the book. I recognised the chains and patterns. They were similar to those I had seen once in a book of a visiting monk. I pointed to a creature that had wings upon its back and flames at its mouth. She smiled.

'It's a dragon,' Jehan said.

My mother looked up and grunted with annoyance.

'We are going now. You know where we are if you want us.'

Jehan spoke to the woman and then we bade our farewells and he accompanied us to the gate.

'Don't be surprised if you get a visit from one of her family,' he said.

'If they come to order me about they will have no luck with any gown, they'd do better to find one of their own.'

'But you are known to be the finest seamstresses.' Then he turned to me saying, 'Roisín, I was sorry to hear of the loss of your husband. Please take this bread, to ease your journey home.'

Accepting the bread, my mother thanked him for his recommendation and then we went on the long road home.

After the visit to the town my mother became restless. I heard her talking to my sister, Eimear, about the fine house she'd seen and the fires and the food. With our father gone and my sister married, there were only my mother and I left. For herself she needed no comfort, but

1319

for me she said she wanted an easier life. It was only a matter of time before we would be moved on again.

The O'Byrnes were known for being a peaceable clan, apart from the ongoing feud with Lord Sutton. Conn O'Byrne had been head of the family for many years and we lived at a safe distance from our neighbours, the O'Tooles, to whom we were related, and beyond those were the O'Dympseys and Kinsellas, both of whom were too busy fighting each other to bother us. We didn't seek out war although to live without it hasn't been known since long before the time of Finn. When the elders talked of the town behind the walls they did so with suspicion: 'To lie down in dwellings with strangers either side of you, to walk daily among people not made of your own blood, it's not natural, not safe.'

It wasn't safe either for a lady from the town to roam outside the walls but it was a test my mother put to the foreigner. If she wanted the dress badly enough, she'd travel and she'd have to want it desperately, there was always the threat of a beast or of wicked men out to destroy life and all else that is good.

Wet week followed wet week and many times we got soaked to the bone. My mother hated the steam that rose from our drying clothes. She complained bitterly and reminisced about the old days, when they had a separate hut made of stone for drying clothes with the fire going all day; when there had been apple trees with red juicy apples from Lughnasa to Samhain; when there had been a road built of wide cut oaks that kept you out of the floods and mud in the winter time; in a place that was surrounded by the thickest ditches of blackthorn and redthorn, planted by her ancestors, until the strangers destroyed it with fire.

The ancient chieftain, our ancestor Bran O'Toole himself, set the foundation pillar of the clan deep in the earth at the entrance to the rath. In later years, in the great hall of that rath, where people gathered and prayed, was kept hidden a relic of Laurence O'Toole. I was never in the original home of my family which lay to the north east of where we finally built again, the third time we settled. For a long time my mother spoke about going back home, even though home existed only in her memory.

I think she has passed this sickness of the heart on to me. I could never look at our rath without comparing it to what we lost and now Tomás is lost too. And so it is never going to be home to me now. It's the place where we were driven to and home will always be the place we were driven from.

One still day, at the end of those wet weeks, a shout went up that strangers were coming. It was a group of mercenaries and among them a figure that I knew immediately to be Cateline.

'Hold yourselves,' my mother said to Conn and the men. 'This party has business with my daughter and me.'

Foreigners were seldom seen in our camp and association with them would lend my mother both power and suspicion. I admired the cloak, the shoes, the horses, but not as much as I admired the strength of courage it took to come here.

1319

By the time they had left us, Bríon had already made a song about them. Bríon, my foolish poet. The same river runs through our veins. We shared our childhood and survived famine together. My mother said we should have married but he loved an O'Dalaigh, the sister of his foster brother, and it was his good fortune to marry her. His marriage marked the end of our close friendship, but his gift of song remained the music of my youth and his laughter the music of my heart.

As I got older I started to dream as though through the eyes of animals. I saw things I'd rather not have looked upon. The savagery of a fox through the eyes of a hare or the cruelty of a hound through the eyes of a badger. I never mentioned this thing to anyone but Bríon, and now he had my secrets and I could no longer talk about them. If he ever told his wife she never let on.

As the nights stretched out and the darkness closed in I was afraid of what I might see in my dreams. I had no one now to talk to about it. It drove me to prayer.

Cateline returned for a final time. One of the men of her party was wounded on the way. Not a mile from our door they were set upon by thieves. Although the men won the fight, her servant, Feilim, was bitten by a hound. Cateline was upset with concern for the boy and it disturbed my mother to see her so. We gave him oatmeal and honey in warm milk as a cure for the shock. By the time the evening was over, Conn had invited the men to the big hall of his home where they drank and feasted, their laughter raucous and the music lively.

Rose

When Jehan offered to provide accommodation for us in a dwelling within the yard of his own property, until the dress was finished, my mother accepted. We went with him despite the silent disapproval of our own people, although they sent us on our way beseeching God to keep between us and all harm.

I called to bid my cousin Bríon and his family farewell but they were abroad. I left them a blanket I'd made of wool with a linen lining. As I laid it on the sleeping mat I prayed for warmth and safety for them all. I left with my mother as if walking in the body of another and the distance between the hills and us quickly grew so that my family lands were soon out of sight.

In the town the wonders were ever unfolding. Jehan installed us in a small dwelling in the courtyard of his house. His own house seemed large for a man with no family that I knew of. There were two rooms close to the ground and an elaborate ladder ascended to even more accommodation. One room had a large fireplace and many pots, where the meals were prepared. This was strange to us who were used to sharing our heavy pots and cooking our main meals over the same fire, or beneath the same hot stones in the cook house. The cloth merchants who bought and sold came from far and wide. The cloths they brought were of such variety and colour that my hands and eyes could not let go of them. Softest reds and golds and even purples. Wools and threads and an array of tools that made the work a pleasure. The servants of the merchant were less than amiable and were suspicious of us. It was hard

1319

to make ourselves understood by the housekeeper and the young man who tended to Jehan and the house. The girl servant, Molly was like us but she was from the far south of the land and spoke a different dialect. As time went on I began to understand her. She told me she was bought by a trader, near her own home and sold into the house as a young child. Her family, being without food, exchanged her for sustenance. She was a *cumal*, an unfree woman, like so many among my people and the foreigners. Morning and evening the girl brought us breakfast and dinner. This unsettled me. We'd have preferred to take care of ourselves. On one occasion the housekeeper, Jeanine, brought us larks to dine on. It was an effort to explain to her that the O'Byrnes were forbidden to eat songbirds by a law that went back to the time of Etain. After this Jeanine took against us and stopped talking to us.

My mother and I worked day and night on the wedding gown. Each button was embroidered and along the hem was a pattern I made from the images I'd seen in the book. I lingered over the design of the shawl. In Cateline's home was a drawing of the sea filled with vessels under flocks of seabirds. I had never seen the sea but I had heard it described in our own stories and songs. I took the dance of the water and stitched it into the woollen shawl. Although she was a devout woman, I stitched the symbols of fertility and the leaf of the holly onto the lining in deep green and red threads.

When we were finished, I didn't need to wait to see Cateline's response to know that we had created something of great beauty. I was so proud, as if I were the one destined to wear it. In the days before the wedding, Jehan accompanied us back and forth with quiet dignity, as if we were his family. As if he were my brother. With the lady he was courteous but not subservient. He held himself as equal. It was this that I admired most about him, the way he treated the women around him. Never a lewd look or rough movement or slight word.

When I held the shawl to the sun, outside our own dwelling, for a final scrutiny of my handiwork, Jehan's face was lit in wonder.

'I knew it would be marvellous, it has gone beyond my dull imaginings.'

His dark brown eyes met mine. He made me feel so pleased that my face reddened. My mother said afterwards, 'Even this man, who has seen the finest garments from far-off lands, admires your work.' Molly was enthralled by the gown and exclaimed it looked like the work of the good people. My mother gave her a clout on the ear for talking aloud about the Sídhe. 'We have enough to contend with, without bringing trouble to the door. Shut your trap!'

Cateline was overjoyed and pressed upon me to explain the patterns to her. 'O Roisín, you have turned me into a queen,' she said. She insisted that I add a rose to the shawl. 'That's your name signed now,' she said. For the rest of my time in the town I took on the name she'd given me, Rose.

We were well rewarded for our work with coin and feast and on the morning we were due to return home, Jehan visited us.

'I have seen the things you can do. If there is no pressing need for

1319

you to return to your own lands, perhaps you might stay a while here?

My mother said we would have to consider it and we walked the road to the monastery, giving alms and employing a monk to pray for us.

'If I'm to stay here,' my mother said, 'You must marry the merchant. I see the way he looks at you and hear the way he speaks to you. In this town we are strangers ourselves and there are not too many of our own people here. Marriages are important. It will provide us with a home, food in our bellies and, God willing, children.'

I trusted her judgement. She was pleased with the proposal. Jehan's last wife had died in childbirth leaving him a widower again. I negotiated my own bargain with him. Whatever profits my mother and I made were to remain with us. He agreed.

We had a small wedding on a fine morning in early autumn and I became Rose Darcy. Jehan's brother and his sister-in-law were present and with them was a daughter of Jehan's who, until that day, neither I nor the household, had knowledge of. Her name was Adeline. She was a tall child with raven black hair and the dark complexion of her father. How could I not have known of her? Among our people all is known. I put it to my new husband that she could live with us, but he said she was settled where she was and her aunt was a mother to her this half dozen summers.

We had sent word to the chieftain of our family, Conn, that I was to be married to the merchant and he returned a gift with the messenger. In this way I knew I had his blessing although it must have irked him to

Rose

lose us to the town.

The memory of Tomás was sweet and sad and I gave my sorrow to the ancestors in the usual way. I drank from the holy well for nine mornings at dawn and with a stone I etched marks along the lines that were already carved in the rock. I then took the holy water and sought out the greatest oak tree I could find and, saying the names of my ancestors, I poured the water onto its base, to nourish the roots of all trees and to honour all the gods who nourish our own roots and make us strong.

Jehan was as much a man of honour as his father before him. My mother and I moved into the main hall of his dwelling. Everything was different for us then. The beds we slept on were stuffed with goose down, the table we sat at was polished and the food we ate was abundant with beef, oysters and poultry. There was a change too in the way the household treated us. I could have been forgiven for comparing it with heaven itself. My mother warned me that comfort comes and goes but I knew she was impressed too.

When word of our work got to the nuns in Grane, Mother Isolde herself came to see us. She asked us to show her our stitching and said it was very fine.

Everyone knew the nuns from Grane. They had land in the town and beyond and they were well thought of. At market day their mead, pickles, cheeses and jams were in demand. When the town was burnt to the ground by the Bruces, it was to the nunnery at Grane that the people

1319

went and it was there they stayed until their homes were rebuilt.

Mother Isolde was accompanied by a young novice, Sister Bertha, and requested that we teach the young woman our method of dress making. My mother, being an astute tradeswoman, said that we would have to think about it as it would require time and instruction on our part and it might interrupt our own business. Mother Isolde offered a payment in return for our instruction and my mother agreed that Sister Bertha could observe and learn from us.

Bertha was a diligent seamstress and made a study of our methods. She spoke the language of the merchants. She resided at the nuns' house in town and spent her days with us. The houseboy, Elias was deeply impressed by her. He found excuses to spend time at the long table with us, until my mother would send him away. Bertha and he could be seen walking together in the evenings before curfew. In the end, my mother sent word to Mother Isolde and Bertha was taken back to the nunnery. There was no objection from my mother about Elias, but we didn't want to find ourselves on the wrong side of the nuns. Cateline had told us that they were a very powerful force in the town.

We kept our own counsel. The ways of people and the town were still a mystery. Jehan's house wasn't far from the Parliament building and, when trials were in session or after a sentence was handed down, we were often witness to both the crowds and the punishments. At times the taunts and shouts of great numbers gathered against a shared enemy were deafening.

Rose

Most common were fines imposed if animals escaped and damage was done. Occasionally thievery and cheating were the charges and these were punished either by fines, by whipping or by being dragged through the town. If the crime was done by a man of standing, more often than not he would be sent to a cell in the Priory for a time that was decided by the judge.

On one occasion I saw a slip of a girl, almost naked and badly beaten, dragged behind a horse.

'Celine, the adulteress,' the men were shouting, 'give us a smile,' and the women were howling at her like wolves. Celine had been caught with a man, not her husband. It was a pitiful sight. I recognised the face of the girl as one of the baker's family. I looked for Mathew, the baker, among the crowds but didn't see him. Celine was bleeding from wounds on her head, her back and her breast. The crowds stood in lines on either side of the road as she was hauled along.

Occurrences like hangings were impossible to avoid in the town. The gossip was incessant and the interest in watching a man swinging until the life was squeezed out of him was irrepressible. The shoemaker had assured me that they were rare events but there were three hangings during the six months we were there.

The first was a young boy who had caused an injury to his master with a knife. The shoemaker told me that the master of the boy was a cruel man. One day, while hunting badgers, the master sent the brother of the boy to lure the badger from the set. The badger raced out to defend itself and was set upon by the hounds. In the foray, the boy was

1319

injured beyond repair and died of his wounds that very night. The boy's brother, in a fit of rage, took a knife and drove it into the chest of the master. Unfortunately, he didn't do damage enough to kill him and he was given the ultimate punishment for his crime. It was an icy day when the boy was hanged and his body was displayed for three days. On the second morning, his hair was iced white as if he had, overnight, turned to old age.

The other two men that were hanged that time were both involved in the crime of stealing from Lord Fitzjohn. I will never forget their screams and the jeers of the town as the ropes went around their necks. In the crowd I saw two women that I took to be their family standing apart from the people. They didn't look at the men and their hands were joined in prayer. They were praying no doubt for God to intervene and rescue the men. When the men screamed, the women fell to their knees. I asked Our Lady to go to their aid, so helpless and pathetic did they appear. The elderly innkeeper's wife helped them to their feet and then ushered them away in the direction of *The Garter Inn*.

Those desperate figures came between me and my sleep for many nights. My mother chastised me and said that it was easier by far to see a stranger hanged than it was to see your own father's head stuck on a spike.

The friends of Cateline employed us and paid us well. My idea of stitching images of dragons onto our dresses appealed to them. My mother resented the women, who she said had never known a hungry day, but I didn't view them as she did. In many ways they were like us.

Rose

They needed food and shelter like ourselves and, depending on which family you were born into, you might be a slave or a king. We had more money now than we needed and we secreted away the greater part of it. We might be glad of it in the future, we said.

Every night with Jehan was as warm as our wedding night. He made me feel as if I were made of gold. He would lie on the bed and ask me to stand naked before him; he said it was to admire me. I said it was a sin to admire false idols and he said that venerating my breasts was worth any penance he would have to do. His touch was tender and he loved to kiss every part of my body. He called me his *amour*.

For six months we all lived like lords. A winter passed and we barely noticed the cold. My mother, whose limbs used to trouble her, grew younger. I made a trip to a healer beyond the walls for help to conceive. Many times my husband had spilled his seed within me but as yet no baby had been conceived.

Jehan was a devoted husband and in my mind's eye I will always see him thus, asleep and contented in the light of the fire. As spring was turning, the first I'd spent in the town, Jehan was attacked outside Dublin, his goods ransacked and he was injured so badly that he slipped away from me. He died in the house of his brother.

For days I'd waited for his return; every hoof I'd heard on the cobbled street sounded like his horse. Every time the door opened I'd expected him to walk through it. Then a messenger was sent to us, and when I heard what had happened, all came falling down around me.

1319

Even now, after all this time, the heartache is deep. How his mind would have turned to me in his final moments, to our hopes of children and to all our plans for a long life together. In my naivety I had hoped that the killings and raids that I'd seen growing up were behind me. Will there never be an end to the savagery of evil men?

The matters of the house were not straightforward. We had no knowledge of the affairs that govern the town. In our own laws, by right the property of my husband should fall to the clan whereupon the chieftain and the elders consider the dependents and the means available and portion it out accordingly. Conn, the chieftain, never failed to do what was right and his father before him was the same. In truth the women in the family were good-hearted and fair-minded and the men took heed of their wisdom in all matters of that kind. In the end, unity of the clan is stronger than division.

But after Jehan's death his brother, Edmond, appeared and claimed that the business and the house now belonged to him. He was a close friend of the Governor of the town and, without Jehan there to interpret for us, it was difficult to understand exactly what was being said or why decisions were being made. Cateline, who had been so good to us, intervened and informed us that by their law I was entitled to a third of the wealth of my husband. With this knowledge I was able to negotiate with Edmond and in the end provision was made for us. I had to take the words of the Governor and Edmond in relation to the amount I was due but it seemed to me a high enough figure and I accepted it.

Rose

We moved back to the smaller dwelling in the courtyard and continued to do our work but soon Edmond began to demand payments from us and increased the cost of the cloths he supplied. He complained to the Governor in the town that we were trading without paying dues to any guild. He had sacked the young man, Elias, who had taken care of Jehan, and Molly told us he was working in Grane now. She said that Edmond was a bad-tempered man, despite his wealth, and that he had on occasion forced himself onto her. When she told us the details of these attacks, my mother swore that she would find a way to put a stop to his gallop.

Early one cold, bright spring morning a knock upon our door startled us. It was Edmond hammering. His voice was raised and for a moment I thought of keeping the door shut against him. My mother grabbed the fire iron and opened the door. He stumbled into the house.

'I demand this house back. There's a woman who is to live here and I want the house for her.'

His speech was drunken and loud. He grabbed me and roughly put his hand on my breast. My mother held the iron at him.

'You have crossed my threshold uninvited. You'll have no luck here or anywhere. Your mind will grow weak and your body will cause you pain. Before the moon is full again, you won't know day from night. You'll drink and it will never quench your thirst and you'll eat and it will never satisfy your hunger. You'll have lust and your manhood will not stand erect again.'

She said all this in our own tongue but he knew by the tone of her voice and the venom in her expression that he was being cursed. Drunk as he was, he grew afraid and let go of me. He slunk back out the door. I had never witnessed my mother using the power of her curse before, although I have always known it was hers to use. It was handed down to her by her mother. After Edmund left her shoulders dropped, she stoked the fire and then slumped in the chair. Her face was tired. It was as if the curse had taken away her own strength. 'We have to move on from here, daughter.' I rubbed her hands and helped her to bed where, despite the daylight, she slept and didn't waken until the following morning.

'We'll come to be slaves here or else we'll die at the hand of that man,' my mother advised. I missed the comfort that we had enjoyed in the main house, but the smaller dwelling was warm and better than conditions in our rath. We missed our family and lands but the work here was a benefit to us in a way that was beyond anything we could have imagined and the relative peace of the town was a seductive friend. We spoke to Cateline and gave thanks again for her knowledge and wisdom.

'You have some wealth of your own now. You could rent your own dwelling,' she said. She told us that there was an agriculturalist who had dwellings at the edge of the town, down near the Abbey. He might agree to rent one to us, she said, and she undertook to speak to the Governor, Edmond and the agriculturalist. It was not usual for a native person to rent in the town but with my name now changed to a foreign name and with the support of Cateline and other women like her, it was granted to

Rose

us. Between her husband and our new landlord, they drew up papers. We would pay rent to the agriculturalist twice yearly; at Easter and on the feast of Saint Michael. She directed us towards a carpenter, Patrick, who would make repairs to the dwelling that had been unoccupied for some time. She changed our lives with the wisdom she showed us and we trusted her judgement on all matters pertaining to life in the town.

I couldn't understand how living could cost so much in coin. At home we lived with little thought of money. We gathered food provided by the earth; we sowed and harvested crops together, we took care of each other and of the animals. We slept under our own roofs; we built our own homes from the ground and the woods. We helped each other, we protected each other and we asked for nothing in return. The ordinary clothes of the family, we made and mended. It was only for the extraordinary occasions like weddings and in very hard times that we relied on coin. For these occurrences we traded whatever we had.

The land towards the Abbey Gate was rocky. The Abbey itself was still undergoing repairs after the burning by the Bruces some years before. All day we could hear the masons working on it. It was almost done, they said, another year would see it complete. Over the months we saw the walls creeping towards the sky. Patrick dug the earth in our new home and covered it with flag stones and Brother James blessed it. We had our own piece of green ground behind our new house and on it we put hens and geese. Geoffrey, the miller's son, our new neighbour, agreed to grow and tend vegetables for us, for a fee. We continued our work in the dwelling of the courtyard until the house was completed,

1319

although now, for every transaction we did, we were under oath to pay an amount of the coin to the Governor. We traded weekly at the market like the others from the town. We became good at counting and our minds became good with remembering the amounts paid out and paid in. We then had to go to the Governor's man in the Parliament Building, who would write down an account of our trade and take what was due for the Governor. In this way, with the good reports of our work from the foreign women, with renting our own dwelling and the paying of taxes, we became accepted by most of the townspeople.

Chapter 6
Brother John
St John's Priory, Tristledermot, 1297 - 1304

The Priory has been my home since the spring that followed the death of my brother. That day has played in my mind like a tune that one hears over and over. I can still see the horses galloping and the flames leaping from the roofs of our neighbours. I can hear the shouts of men as spears are driven through their bodies.

My brother is high upon a black horse, held firmly by a wild Irish warrior. This struggling child can't be Alvery, I think, and yet I know it is. The riders gallop through the open gate and although there must be noise – the thatch is burning and people are crying – I hear only the silence left in their wake.

Seven days after he was taken, my mother was walking in the town. The people were thatching their roofs and mending what they could. A sack was flung over the wall and a shout went up, striking fear of another attack. The sack landed with a cold thud at my mother's feet. She stood and stared at what had spilled from the sack. At first she perceived only a heap of cloth. She bent to pick up the bundle and slowly realised that it was the body of her son, bloodied and maimed. His fair hair was matted and coloured brown with his own blood. His clothes were in tatters and his blue eyes were gone from their sockets. I heard her howling that morning and thought that it was the sound of a wild animal dying slowly, caught in one of the traps beyond the wall.

She was carried home with Alvery. When she was able, she bathed his dead body and dressed it. I watched all from the loft where Alvery and I had slept all our lives together. His empty eye sockets turned my stomach and stayed in my mind all my life. We had a funeral and buried my brother. My chest felt the weight of every piece of earth that was thrown into his grave.

I recall again and again those cold mornings in our dwelling. The roof was unfixed for a time, the fire remained unlit and the sound of my mother's feet, usually so light, dragged over the flagstones. She spoke as if to my brother, holding his bedding to her face.

'I'm going home little one; this land is worse than the one we left. I'm sorry now we left it. These warring tribes will kill us all. I'm sorry, my pet, my fair haired darling, O God, my God, my God!'

She said these things but I knew she didn't mean them. She didn't really want to leave me. My father and I were quiet in our own separate ways. Then my voice and my hearing disappeared and my mother, who had taught us how to read, made letters for me from rushes. I learned to arrange them to say anything I needed and in return she spoke to me in letters. I missed the sound of her laughter, my father's voice, my brother's giggles but most of all I missed the birds in the morning. I never knew quite when the day had begun.

There's much of that time that I don't remember. Everything was different. We had become a different family. When I did my tasks, or found a shiny blade, there was nothing to boast about and no one I could impress. The neighbours called me but I couldn't hear them and so they stopped speaking to me. My mother was frightened all of the time and her eyes changed. I stumbled about trying to be two people, wanting to disappear, wanting to be seen, aching for the time before everything changed. I spent my days tending the vegetables, the hens and the sheep which were indifferent to my silence.

Four seasons passed. I became good with letters. A monk arrived late one evening from a far-off town and he was treated in the manner that was customary. Everyone knows that offering kindness to a stranger is good for curing sorrow. The monk spoke to me but my mother pointed to my ears and shook her head. His face was gentle, full of kindness. She beckoned me to her and wrote the words of his speech for me. He watched me arrange letters for my own words and then asked me if I had devotion to any saint. I wrote 'Saint John' and the monk seemed pleased with this. His clothes were heavy, deep blue and woollen, with a red cross on his chest. The monk said I was clever because I was good with letters and this made me very happy. He said I might one day become a scribe, a holy man who writes words for the world to read and, although I didn't know what that meant, for the first time in a long time, my heart skipped with joy.

My mother's head was low but her eyes were gleaming with tears and something else too. When my father came home he had in his arms a pile of wood which he threw into the fire. It blazed in a way that was strange. He sat me upon his knee and I knew he was singing the song that he always sang. He smelled of the woods and the earth and the

Brother John

smoke and I inhaled all of it. Enough to last a lifetime. The next morning, I left my family and started my life with the monks.

I missed my parents but no more than I missed my brother. The monastery was a busy collection of stone buildings outside the town of Tristledermot. The days were punctuated by prayers and rules and yet there was time to play. There were other boys there too and it wasn't long before I made new friends. At the other end of the town, where the Abbey was situated, was an enormous pond abundant with fish that could be seen jumping and splashing all the day long. Nothing made us happier than an errand that took us by that pond.

When I spoke with Brother Francis about the Abbey he said that unlike the Crouched Friars like himself, those at the Abbey did not live by the rules of poverty of St Augustine and that their fish pond was excessive and should, by rights, feed the poor of the land. All the same he sometimes sent me on a quiet task to purchase some of the privileged trout from Simon, the man who took care of the pond.

The Priory was alive with animals. Goats, hens, geese, cows, doves became our companions and alongside these, the company of other boys and the lessons, I was contented.

Brother Francis was committed to making me and another boy, Martin, into the best scribes he could. I learned a new way of praying and a peace settled on me when I was first allowed to put ink on parchment. In the room of the scribes, the scriptorium, I could forget my broken ears, as all was very still there, save for the small movements needed to make words and beautiful drawings.

I loved the work, despite the awkward position it demanded from my body. It was an escape from the world. Each letter on the page was a task so absorbing that a morning could pass quickly. A mistake could lead to a thump on the arm or a slap on the head: parchment was precious. Brother Francis showed me the work of the scribes and copyists and on one occasion I saw the Book of Kildare. The illuminated leaves were the most beautiful things I had ever seen. He told me that one day I would learn to illuminate letters and pictures and make holy books. That hope kept me drawing and writing at every opportunity I got.

Sometimes my mother came into my mind, the sadness of her farewell to me and her promise that the monastery would be a safer place for me. If safer meant not hungry, she was right. Most of the monks spoke in a language that was like hers, as well as in Latin. Like us, they called the people who lived out in the woods and beyond the wild Irish. Brother Francis only spoke of the death of my brother once.

It was a warm evening in the garden of the Priory and I had finished the work that had been set for me. I took advantage of the spare moments and lay outstretched on the ground, my back feeling the heat of the earth seep into my small bones. Clouds passed overhead in ever changing shapes. I saw the figure of a dancing cow drift by and smiled happily. Suddenly a man towered above me. Without the use of my ears, I had no forewarning that he was approaching. He was dressed in the clothes of the wild Irish and his hair was long and loose.

Brother John

In terror I sprang up and ran as fast as I could, expecting the man to grab hold of me. Unable to raise the alarm, I locked myself into the cell of Brother Francis and wept. I imagined that the Priory was being ransacked and that all were being slain. I wanted to die with the shame of my cowardice. I could have rung the bell and warned people.

Brother Francis went to retire that night and found his room bolted against him. When I saw his face at the small window I was so relieved that I cried again. He looked unharmed and I opened the door.

He went to a great length the following day to explain to me about the wild Irish in the words that he wrote. He said that the church of the wild Irish was different from our own, and that the Pope in Rome complained that it was too liberal, but that it followed the teachings of Jesus just like we did. He said the man I'd seen was Malachy O'Toole, a patron of the hospital and a good man and that not all people from any group are the same, and that Malachy was not one of the men who'd killed my brother. He said that war was a curse among people. I asked him about the Holy Land, where the Crusaders fought, but he repeated that all war was evil.

For two full years the silence stayed in my ears and for those two years I saw my brother whenever I caught a glimpse of my own reflection. And then I changed as I grew and I no longer saw him in the glass. In my mind's eye, he was at the right hand of St John, who was always before me.

I will never forget the morning in the Priory that I awoke to the sound of the bell ringing. It startled me to such an extent that I fell out of the bed onto the woollen rug. Forgetting to dress and scrambling to my feet, I ran to Brother Francis, who was in deep slumber. I shook him with all my might. Before he opened his eyes, he spoke.

'By God's own bones, what kind of a bricon has me?'

The words made me laugh. His anger subsided when he saw me and heard my laughter.

'God's blessing upon you, boy.'

He smiled then and ruffled my hair.

'You are no fool boy; it's a great morning indeed for all of us.'

He made the sign of the cross and I copied him. We both knelt by his bed and he said a prayer of gratitude to God and to St John for the restoration of both my hearing and my voice.

Shortly after this, on a summer's morning, a commotion from outside the gate quickened my step. An elderly woman was poorly and she had made her way to the Priory before she collapsed at the gate. I helped her to her feet and she leaned on my shoulders in order to walk. She was Irish but she spoke my language. The women in the hospital took her from me. As her health improved she sent for me, the boy who had helped her. In this way I got to know Nuala O'Byrne. She remained too weak to travel and when she was able, she worked in the kitchen.

There were two kinds of sick people who came to the hospital. The first were people like Nuala. Often they were poor and destitute, with no family. The other kind were the lepers who were sent to the hospital and there lived out the rest of their lives. I occasionally saw the lepers. They were contained in a room beside the chapel of Mary Magdalene, apart from all others, to prevent the air becoming corrupted for all of us. The nuns from Grane sent women to help with the sick and the monks provided for them too.

Every morning before the sun rose, the lepers walked around the circular path at the far end of the hospital. Brother Francis warned us to stay away from them. He said leprosy was a disease of the soul and that only the holiest people could take care of the lepers without fear. Martin, my fellow scribe, who was fascinated by the deformities of the lepers and by the women who cared for them, found a place to hide where we were concealed. Their limbs were incomplete and rotting. Their faces were misshapen. When the physician came to bleed them, they could be heard crying. I went with Martin on just two occasions but I found the sight too pitiable to look on.

Apart from the lessons and taking care of the animals, I helped with the beehives and drew water from the well for the cook. Whenever he caught me, he always found a task for me and I learned the skill of baking from him. I was often in the kitchen.

Nuala cooked food that I had never before tasted and she had the most wondrous faery stories. These stories kept my belly burning at night and I thought of them often during the day. I had to swallow my tongue to stop myself telling Brother Francis about them. We were under oath not to tell any stories other than those from the bible. Brother Francis said that many of the wild Irish were pagans still and I knew he'd put an end to the faery stories and Nuala's employment if he ever found out. He had no interest in faeries.

Brendan arrived at the Priory more than two years after me. We were of a similar age but he seemed much older. His voice was deepening early, he was strong and he knew things that I had never heard of. He knew how to hunt rabbits and hares, and which berries and plants could be eaten. He spoke the language of the wild Irish and he taught it to me. It was unlike Latin or English, but I loved the sound of the words he spoke. As the months went on, he told me more stories of the Sídhe and tales that made my hair stand on end.

He told me about the great warriors of the Fianna and Finn Mac Cumhail and he fashioned a stick for me that we used to hit stones with. He could always hit the stones further than I could. Whenever I managed a good shot he called me Cú Chulainn, which was a name in an old story in which a boy called Setanta killed a hound and then, as compensation to the hound's master, did the work of the hound and thus became known as Culainn's hound.

One moonlit night when we were in the dormitory, Brendan woke me. I followed him outside.

'It's a great night for eel fishing,' he said.

'If Brother Francis catches us, we will be whipped,' I told him.

'No one will ever know, the river far beyond the Priory has eels. If we hear anyone we'll hide and we'll be back before the bell rings.'

He gave me holy water and told me to keep it with me in case the

Brother John

good people were abroad.

'And if any of them speaks to us, don't you talk to them. I'll do the talking. They can trick you into all kinds of things if you don't know what to say. And whatever you do, don't tell them your name.'

Alvery would have loved Brendan and this adventure. The moon put a silver hue on everything it touched. The road to the river was long and in the distance the river shone ahead of us for ages, never seeming to get closer. I told Brendan this and he said it was a trick of the river god. We weren't the only fishermen out that night, so we crept up river until the others were out of sight and sound and we were alone with the river in the silvery light.

Brendan told me to pick reeds from the marshy land beside us. He disappeared behind a clump of trees and returned with something in his hands.

'What is that?'

'It's an eel cage, you ludramon!'

He wove the rushes into the basket, to mend a hole. The cage was wide and tall at one end and narrowed down to an opening. The rushes were threaded in tiny lattices between willow rods.

'Take off your clothing or it'll get wet, and sit there on that stone. Don't move until I tell you.'

I sat on the cold stone and watched Brendan squat in silence by the edge of the river, his head tilted downwards slightly. His face was lit brightly in the moonlight. The night air was damp and a mist was draped over the soggy land ahead. Frogs croaked and a small creature squealed as it met its end. I hoped it was an owl and not a wolf that killed it. Brendan stood and held a coin to the moon and then tossed it into the water.

'What are you doing?' I whispered.

He held his finger to his lips.

'I'm trying to tell where the eels are.'

'But your eyes were closed, how can you see?'

'Be very quiet and watch this.'

He disrobed and waded into the river, the water almost waist high. He continued until he found a shallow place.

'Get in, come on.'

I stepped in, the cold caused me to catch my breath. My feet sank into the muddy bed. Tiny pinkeens darted against my legs. I tried not to think about pike.

Brendan placed the trap in the water and then handed it to me.

'Bury the end of it in the silt.'

The cage was almost the width of the narrow part of the river. He walked upstream, crouched low, his arms in the water and then, silently, turned towards me again. As he neared I felt something brush past my legs, and then something splashed.

'Ease up the cage now, slowly,' Brendan whispered.

And sure enough as I lifted it out of the water, the trap was heavier than it had been and something was moving in it. Brendan took it from me and pressed the open end against his chest. Once it was clear of the water, the creature inside thrashed violently. Brendan rolled himself and the cage onto the bank and clutched it.

'If it gets out, it'll slide back into the river.'

I climbed up after him. Brendan was swan-coloured under the moon. The cage was still and Brendan was laughing.

'Did you see that? Wasn't it fierce?'

We repeated this method many times but our net was full just twice more.

We dressed and both made our way back to the path that would take us home. Brendan took the last eel from the basket. It was a large creature, long and dark. He handed all of them to me as he concealed the basket again. I was hoping they were truly dead. He wrapped the three in cloth.

'What were you doing with the coin?' I asked.

It was unheard of to throw silver away.

'It was an offering to the god.'

'Which god?'

'The river god.'

'Is that not blasphemy?'

'No, that's a different thing. It's bad luck not to offer it.'

'You mean the river is a god?'

'Yes.'

'What about Our Lord?' I said.

'There's no denying Our Lord, don't be a ludramon,' he said.

I didn't understand what he said.

'And how did you see the eels? Your eyes were closed.'

'If you keep pestering me I won't take you fishing again. Did you see the size of these?'

It was almost light when we got back. We left the eels in the cook house. Brendan said that Nuala would be glad of them. We weren't to know that the head cook would discover them or that he would report their presence to the Prior.

Later in the day, drowsy with tiredness in the scribe's room, I saw Brendan through the open door. His clothing was folded down from his body and he was naked from the waist up. A tangle of thorny briars was wrapped around him and the Prior was addressing him. There was blood weeping from the scratches on his chest, back and shoulders.

I made an excuse to leave and found Nuala in the cook house. She brought me to the side of the salt house and said crossly,

'What in God's name were you thinking? I know you were with him, you ludramon. The cook marched straight to the Prior, as he was sure that the eels were taken from the Abbey pond.'

'But they didn't come from the Abbey pond. They came from further up the river, way beyond the town.'

'That's even worse, wandering the land at night, you could have both been killed or kidnapped or worse.'

Nuala was disgusted with me. Her voice was trembling and her hand was pinching my arm. I couldn't help the tears that came. When she saw this, she relaxed her grip.

'O, it's natural for children to want to run amok. But you have no idea of the things that can happen to a child.'

Brother John

With this the tears flowed freely and I blurted out.

'I do, Nuala, I do know what can happen.'

She softened completely then and held me to her. She rubbed my hair and my back. My shoulders shook as I sobbed and the snot from my nose ran onto her neck.

'A mo cuisle, my poor boy, it's for your own good that I'm sharp with you.'

The tears eventually stopped and Nuala took me into the salthouse where she was curing ham and gave me salt to rub into the flesh of the pig. Within a short time I had forgotten my tears and I quizzed her about the river and the god-people.

'Is the river a kind of god?' I asked her.

'It's an old story; the river takes life, it gives life, it holds life. Without the river, there is no life. But it's not a god anymore and don't let Brother Francis hear you asking that. Brendan is filling your head; he'll get in more trouble for that if anyone hears you. Now clean the salt from your hands and run back to the hall.'

When I was a boy in the monastery there were always pilgrims but two festivals in particular each year brought people to us in great numbers – the feast of St Brighid in February and the feast of St John the Baptist in June. There was great excitement among us young people during the festivals. We didn't mind the extra work they brought us. Brother Francis used to tell us to treat everyone as if they were our own family and this always stirred happiness in me.

It was on the feast of St Brighid, ten years after I first arrived in St

John's, when I met with the holy man who would inspire me to travel beyond the confines of the Priory and further still to lands overseas.

It was a cold spring day. People had been travelling all night in order to arrive in time for Saint Brighid's Day. Even the wild Irish came for this feast. They camped outside the town walls, not having the means or inclination to go within. The Priory was set outside the walls and because the monks visited their clans, and because the O'Tooles were patrons of the Priory, they were less suspicious of us than they were of the Franciscans in the Abbey at the other side of the town.

After I took my vows, I used to assist the Prior when he baptised the children of the clans. Their hospitality always touched me. What they had, they shared with us. I became familiar with their music, their children, and with the names of the families of the area.

They came with gifts, in gratitude for surviving another winter and to ask for protection for the year ahead. There was a monk among them, tall, weathered and with eyes so blue it was as if they contained the summer sky. Unlike our tonsured heads, his hair was thick and long. I felt a pull towards this man as if my Lord were guiding me to him. His clothes were worn and heavy and all around him a warm peace settled, a sign of a Godly man.

The gifts of food that the pilgrims brought were added to our own offerings and after a long day of fasting and prayer, we provided a banquet on behalf of St Brighid to sustain the souls of all who attended. The long tables were set in rows and the young monks and kitchen workers distributed the food into the waiting bowls of the pilgrims.

Brother John

Many brought mead and wine and of this we kept a quantity for the sick in the hospital. The rest we gave away, which made for satisfied pilgrims who were willing to share their stories.

I saw the old monk again as he was waiting his turn to eat. In the gesture of a generous heart, he encouraged those around him to go before him. Seeing my chance to meet him, I took his bowl and filled it.

'A thousand thanks, young monk, for your kindness.'

He spoke in the language of my mother and wore the red cross of the order. I realised he was one of our visiting brothers from France. His words meant more to me than all the prayers that day.

Later still, after the evening prayers, I found him sitting quietly in contemplative silence. I stayed near him and a stillness fell that was deeper than anything I had hitherto known.

In my mind's eye, as if dreaming, I saw a vast expanse of water that can only have been the sea of which my mother used to speak. I saw people of different colours, all with maladies and troubles. I saw the hands of this man touch them and heal them and then his hands became mine and the vision frightened me. I opened my eyes wide and the man was watching me.

'You will travel the world young man,' he said.

His smile had the heat of fire in it. I was brimming with love for all my fellow men.

His name was Brother Gabriel and he told me of his travels in the great world overseas. He had bathed in the river Jordan and prayed in the Garden of Gethsemane. I was beside myself with excitement when he said he'd stood on the road where Jesus had been crucified. It was as if I were speaking to one of the true apostles.

'Were you not afraid of the fighting? And of the Saracens?' I asked him.

'If you want to travel in the Holy Land, you must rely on Saracens. One of my greatest companions was a Turk. We thought we'd find a safe pilgrim path in the Holy Land.'

'Wasn't that what the Templars used to do? Didn't they help people through the Holy Land?'

'You could get arrested for talking of the Knights Templar these days, young monk.'

'And did you find a safe path?'

'Not that, no. But I did find something else. Now run and fetch me a blanket, young fellow, it's to get cold.'

'But the visiting brothers have a place to sleep in the dormitory.'

'There are a lot of rogues in the world but there are always people who need saving, especially the rogues. I'll be sleeping out here tonight.'

Chapter 7
Rose
Tristledermot, 1319 - 1324

Edmond had little luck once we departed from his courtyard. Sometimes I'd see him as I passed; he was always unkempt in appearance. In the days after we left, he would shout at me.

'There is the crafty whore who stole my brother's wealth.'

I knew if he continued in his taunting, the townspeople would believe him. I was grateful that my mother and I had made a practice of being seen in prayer with regularity and we had paid our tithes. On the other hand, Edmond was never seen in this way and was known to be mean with payments to the church.

I went to see Cateline and told her of it. She said it was an offence to make false accusations and that I could take a case of law against him. This was not my desire. Cateline asked her husband to communicate with the Governor about the incidents. After this, Edmond stopped calling out to me. It was my first victory in the town and I was grateful for the writ that caused him to stop.

Our home was beyond anything we could have imagined before we moved to the town and was bigger than the dwelling in Edmond's courtyard. We had two rooms, one for sleeping, one for cooking and working. Beneath the thatch of the roof lay enormous timber beams from which we hung our lengths of fabric and our belongings. Cateline

Rose

gave us a table and two chairs and Geoffrey, the boy next door, made two small stools for us. Patrick built two wide beds against the walls of the sleeping room and we obtained mattresses stuffed with horse hair. Patrick made shelving and hooks. In both rooms were deep fireplaces set at the base of a chimney and so the smoke travelled upwards and didn't fill the rooms. We had an opening for light with a thin layer of bone inserted as a shield against the wind and rain.

In the green ground at the back of the house stood a shelter for animals with space enough in a loft for storing feed. We had the advantage of being but a short distance from a well. The work remained plentiful and it seemed to me that it always would.

Jeanine, the housekeeper, paid me a visit and informed me that Edmond's wife was ill and that the woman, who he had moved into the house in the courtyard, had died leaving a child behind her. The cook was caring for the baby but asked me if I'd take it.

'It has the blood of your dead husband in its veins. Edmond's blood is the same as his brother's,' she said.

Her words landed on me like a weight. How I would have loved a child of my own. The years were moving and I was approaching a score in number yet I couldn't take the child of Edmond. It would draw him upon us and bind us to him again. I confessed to Father Michael, who said I should ask the Lord for guidance and I prayed each morning for an omen. At the suggestion of my mother, under cover of night, I visited the caileach who lived in the wood, a woman who was known to have the gift of seeing. She warned me against taking the baby, that it would bring misfortune into the house. She told me too that there would be another child who would enter my home before too long, one who would bring happiness to me. I told my mother this and she said that we should take the advice.

The miller's wife, Ava, made ale and kept bees. The miller worked in the monks' mill. Their son, Geoffrey, was enthusiastic in his work on our green ground. He dug it and planted leeks, kale, beans and peas. From the garden of his mother he took plants and cultivated them in ours. He made a fence of hazel rods that separated the animals from the vegetables and he made a large wooden trough that held water for days. His father left early each morning and returned late and we seldom saw him. Ava was generous with the bread she baked and she gave us fine soft bread, such that we had never tasted before, not a trace of grit in it. In return we made a lined woollen blanket for her.

The first years we spent in our new dwelling were productive and peaceful. We often talked of our clan. When news reached us of trouble beyond the walls, my mother sent for my sister, Eimear, and her family.

Eimear had trouble entering the town. Geoffrey came for me saying that a woman claiming to be my sister was at the gate but the guards had pushed her and denied her passage. I hurried to the gate with my purse. Coin can buy many a mind. At the gate the guards and some women were loud in their talk, drunk. When there's trouble beyond the walls there's trouble within, as the guards would often ward off their fears of raids by making cruel sport of innocents. I knew the men by name.

'There's a woman beyond the gate that I'm here to claim.'

'No entry now. The gate is closed for the night. We have orders from the Governor.'

Louis, the man speaking, was the most pliable of the three. He was tall and gentle and often tried to stop the harassment of people by the others. This made him unpopular with the watchmen but liked by the town's people. I was relieved that he was present as the other pair were men of bad character.

'And tell me, Louis, is it an order of the Governor that the guards drink an excess of ale with women, while protecting the people of the town?'

'Watch your mouth, Irisher,' said the second man, Philip.

'I'm not looking for a fight with you. Perhaps some silver will soften your cough. Philip, there's a woman beyond the gate, who is my sister. She's ill. If you leave her out tonight she'll surely die. The Governor won't thank you if I have to call him from his meal in order to prevent you from putting my kin to death. I'll pay the three of you twice the toll you're due.'

Outside the gate there were many camped and their fires burned the length of the road as it was the night before market day. My sister was admitted, weak and exhausted. For a moment I thought there was a mistake, I didn't recognise her but then saw that she had her daughter with her. I spoke to Eimear but she didn't answer. Her fists were tightened on the few belongings she possessed and I held her upright as we made our way home where she collapsed onto the bed. It was clear that Eimear had her fair share of troubles. We were delighted to see Bridín, her daughter, who'd grown so much since we'd left. I will always wonder in this life how so much joy can reside beside so much sorrow.

Eimear slept for days with barely the strength to lift her head. Bridín was weak with the hunger too and we fed them small portions of stirabout and asked the monks to pray for them. Brother James came to our dwelling and anointed Eimear, for we weren't sure if she would survive. We took turns keeping vigil by night and stitched our cloth by day. Not for the first time I admired the strength of my mother. As the weeks passed, by God's grace, Eimear and Bridín recovered.

Little by little the story of what had happened was told. Conn, our chieftain, had received notice from the Archbishop of Dublin, that the land he lived on had been granted by the king to the Archbishop himself, and that the O'Byrnes and the O'Tooles must move off, as it was no longer their land. From now on it was to be used for farming. They were offered a choice – either to leave immediately or stay and become tenant labourers of the Archbishop.

Conn warned our neighbours and all of the men got ready for the fight they knew was coming. There was no chance of winning. The soldiers had weapons unlike anything we had. Their crossbows could shoot arrows with such power that they could pierce metal and enter a man's heart from a great distance. The women with children were sent to hide in the mound, that is the secret chamber dug into the hill, and all

Rose

else stayed and fought bravely.

The mother of Eimear's husband, old Áine the midwife, was on her deathbed at that time and refused to die in any other place.

'If you stay in this bed, you'll be burned alive,' Eimear told her but Áine said she had lived through more than three score of winters, which was as old as anyone could expect to live and old enough to decide where she wanted to spend her last moments.

When Eimear spoke of this, her voice became high as if her throat might stop the words from coming out. My mother rubbed her back as you might comfort a child and Eimear continued. Áine said that she was glad that Eimear's mother was spared this attack.

'I was with your mother the last time we were moved on. Your grandfather was killed that time, a brave strong man cut down short. O Mother of God, pray for us. I've helped every baby of the clan into this world, since I was a girl. I've baptised them and anointed them. I've laid them in their mothers' arms and the ones who didn't live, I placed in the ground with my own hands. I'm done with this life. I've taught you all I know, young Eimear. May God bless the work you do, and may you find your final rest with Him in eternity, when your time comes.'

Eimear had begged Áine to allow herself to be carried away by the men, and spare herself the agony of what was about to happen.

'I'm a good Christian woman, Eimear. These men who are hunting us out are not men of God, and that Bishop is a devil in disguise, no matter what his title. They will all face Judgement when the Last Day comes. Saint Ita is by my side and I am not afraid. Go with the others

1319 - 1324

and take the child. There's hope for you. I'll pray for your safe passage.'

But Eimear didn't go to the mound. She wouldn't leave Áine to die alone. When the houses began to burn and the smoke was thick about them, Eimear and Bridín hid in the earthen hole beneath the flagstone in their dwelling. Old Áine refused to hide. When Eimear last glimpsed Áine, she was praying and peaceful and Eimear said that she hadn't heard her cry out.

My mother and I blessed ourselves when we heard about Áine and, until her own death, my mother devoted her prayers to old Áine and Saint Ita whenever she was troubled.

Those of the clan who could travel went westward. Eimear's own caring, sweet husband was killed by an arrow. She discovered him after the fire was spent. She described all that had happened and all that she had seen and I felt as if I were seeing through her eyes. My heart was heavy with inexpressible sadness.

It was in the hours after the attack that our messenger had found Eimear and told her that her mother had sent for them. Our mother was wretched with guilt. 'If only I had sent for you earlier,' she said. Eimear again and again answered, 'But we couldn't have come to you then; we couldn't have left before the attack.'

All through the town were similar stories of destruction beyond the walls. I heard the people at the market talk about the attack on my family and on other families: the O'Dempseys and the Kinsellas.

'The wild Irish want everything and want to pay for none of it; they're no better than animals. They ate each other during the last big hunger,' the shoemaker said.

He saw me then and added, 'Excepting yourself and your family, ma'am.'

I forced a smile and told him not to mind.

'I heard the same reports about the foreigners when I was a child,' I said. 'But I have yet to meet a man or woman of either kind who admits to it.'

The shoemaker would never understand us. Since I'd first arrived in the town I had never felt more aware of being different than during the time of raids and war. I'd changed my name, worked honestly, paid taxes, given to the religious and the poor, but it would never make me one of them. Not that I wanted that, I just wanted to be considered ordinary.

Back at our dwelling, I was ashamed when I heard my sister speak. Her child was left fatherless while I had slept in comfort among strangers.

Since leaving the clan, I'd imagined life there continuing on in the same way as it always had done. Thoughts of my family filled me with a sense of comfort and love. I could stay in the town but home was where I belonged. I felt incomplete in the town. The foreigners had taken our lands before I was born, and although I'd heard my mother talk of it, I hadn't understood until Eimear's arrival what it felt like. With the destruction of my home, it was as if part of my soul had been torn from me.

The Archbishop's men didn't just want to drive us out, they wanted to cut us down. Bríon, his family, my aunts and cousins, were all gone now. My mother, Eimear, Bridín and myself were four single trees left standing in a felled wood.

I went to confession later that evening and confessed my anger at the shoemaker to Father Michael. It wasn't just at him, I was raging with my neighbours and the soldiers and all of the people of the town. The priest gave me penance and absolved me of my sins but by the time I had returned to our dwelling I was full of fury again. For the sake of my sister I tried to make myself peaceable.

The arrival of people like ourselves in the town had become a regular occurrence since the time we had taken up our dwelling there. Their labour had dug ditches and replanted the Governor's woods that had suffered so much at the hands of the Bruces. The big hunger had forced even more people into the town so after that time there were people from all places within the walls.

At the south gate of the town a bony hand, said to be that of Edward the Bruce, was displayed in a box and people told their children stories of how the Scottish and wild Irish were beaten in the end. Anyone who remembered that time spoke of the damage that was done. I vaguely remember, as a child, the light and black smoke from the burning town, fields and all things alive which fell into the path of the Bruces. In our clan, unlike others, we did not glory in the destruction. It ruined the markets in the towns and, at that time of great hunger, we suffered huge losses ourselves because of this.

Rose

Cateline came to see us. When she entered our dwelling, she wept and held my mother and then myself. She brought some bread and wine and a little figure of a baby made from wood and cloth for the child.

'These attacks on your people are not done by my people,' she said. 'It's a terrible thing to hear such stories about the deaths of families. I thank God that He has spared you and your family in His mercy.'

Although she didn't understand that my mother, Eimear, Bridín and I were just a tiny part of our whole family, her words and kindness washed the anger from me. She told us it was warring that had driven her people from their home in France after the raids had devoured the bulk of them. As she spoke she placed her hands upon her belly and I realised than that she was carrying her own new kin.

I brought Eimear and Bridín to the monastery to be blessed and offered alms on their behalf. Brother James was delighted to see them again and he took them to meet the Abbot, who had the gift of languages. Father Michael tried to talk with Eimear but she was suspicious of all. I was the same way myself when I first arrived. Through her eyes we must appear very much like people of the town.

When a fair day was on the horizon it was as if the spirit of the whole town, and all around it, awakened after a long sleep. Market day happened weekly in the town but there were two fair days in the year, in Bealtaine, the early summer and at Martinmas, in the month before Christmas.

1319 - 1324

Fair day was known for trouble. Guards grew in number. In the days before it, huge groups camped outside the walls with their livestock and wares. Each item they intended to sell was marked by the Governor's men and a toll was charged according to its value. Stalls were erected and cooking pits were dug, lodgings were prepared and activities that were usually kept hidden were on view.

The innkeeper's wife had a long line of visiting nieces; all dressed in a particular style and all were accommodating young women, available as companions to men who might be lonely in their private chambers, in *The Garter Inn*. My mother amused herself by asking me, throughout the days of the fair, how was it that the Governor calculated the toll for the transactions that were exchanged between the innkeeper's nieces and the men.

'Go and ask them yourself.'

But she never did. We never set foot in *The Garter Inn,* although the innkeeper did order from us a dozen aprons, and in doing so prompted other innkeepers to follow suit. We had, by this time, taken to producing blankets, which we embroidered in our traditional way. The demand for our patterns was high and fair day was an opportunity for us to make good bargains. That year we had the help of Eimear and Bridín and the fair was a welcome distraction for all of us.

We set out our stall in the place allotted to us on the Fair Green. From that morning until the next, the music of the foreigners could be heard at every turn. The smell of meat roasting was enough to make mouths water. Badger, boar, swan, cow and every other creature turned above the cooking pits. Furs, the like of which I'd never seen, were in abundance and at the far end of the fair were livestock, waiting to be exchanged for a good price. Peacocks cried out their objections to being caged and, as if in answer, donkeys brayed with deafening stubbornness. Spinning wheels and spindles sat alongside scythes and swords and all manner of things that were not ordinarily available.

The fair swelled with crowds and Brother James took advantage of the day to preach to the flock about temptations of the flesh. I translated some of his words for Eimear.

'If a man lusts after a woman, a sin is committed, and if he acts on his lustful thoughts, it is another and more dangerous sin. If he should kiss her lips, caress her body and gaze upon her for his pleasure, this is yet another cause of sin.'

By now a crowd had gathered around Brother James and he had a twinkle in his eye as he spoke.

'And even if a man has lustful thoughts of his wife, if he is passionately in love with her and distracted by her, if his manhood stands erect whenever he dwells on her naked image, or if he should take her and enter her with no thought of the purpose of procreation and if his seed should spill upon her, and not in her, if he should have only his own satisfaction and deranged pleasure in mind, then St Jerome tells us that this too is a sin. And must be confessed. For, St Jerome says, if the Lord is your master, such passion for any other person, even your wife, is adultery.'

The people standing nearby were cheering now.

'Tell us more, Brother James. What if his seed should spill in her hair? Is this a sin?'

'Fornication of the flesh is a mark on the soul and must be confessed.'

'Would you like us to confess here and now?' Another man asked and the people laughed.

'And if she should enjoy the fornication of her husband. Is this adultery too?'

'Yes, this is most definitely adultery.'

'And if she should lie with a man not her husband and not enjoy it, is this adultery too? Which is the greater sin?'

Brother James gave a merry response to this and the people laughed again. Even Eimear smiled, although both she and Bridín were nervous of the people. It seemed that every foreigner in the land was in the town that day. Amongst the foreigners and those of the town, who were well-dressed and well fed, were people like us – many of them thin and hungry – having been sent by their families to sell whatever possible and bring back food and coin. Eimear wanted to help them all. I explained to her that if we gave all we had, we would have nothing left for ourselves. Then when things were scarce we would go hungry. As I said this, I knew that it was not the way I used to think. In the clan all was used up, in an effort to keep all alive. 'But Eimear this is not the

Rose

clan, there are so many more people here.' All the same, I purchased three loaves of bread for her to divide as she saw fit, and this seemed to satisfy her.

It was late in the evening when we packed what was left of our goods. I was last to leave our stall and darkness had begun to fall over the marketplace. It started to rain, and in an attempt to keep the cloth dry, I held it beneath my cloak, my head bent low. I missed my footing on the slippery ground and almost fell, but a strong arm caught me and righted me. When I looked up I met the dark, deep eyes of the handsomest man I'd ever seen. Despite the dim light I could see every detail of his face. It was as if it glowed of its own accord. I no longer heard the noise of the people from ale houses or the traders shouting to one another. A veil fell over all else save that man. He smiled at me and my soul rushed towards him.

'Let me help you through the mud,' he said.

I took his arm and steadied myself against him. His body was as firm as a mountain. When we reached the square, every window there was lit bright by lamps. I looked upon him again and, for a moment it seemed that he stood in a rainbow.

'What is it?' he asked.

Speech left me. The end of the rainbow swept right through his heart. The colours were rich and pure and I was dizzy at the sight.

'Is there something else I can help you with?'

My hand was still touching his arm. I'd met many men, been twice married, and yet never had I felt so instantly overcome with love.

'You are built like a wall,' I said.

He stared into me and it was as if time had ceased. He laughed lightly.

'Then I have become my own best work,' he said. 'I'm a stonemason.'

We both laughed and enjoyed the happiness we saw in each other. He took my hand and, although his palm was calloused and rough, his touch was like goose down on my skin. He was a foreigner but the name given to him, by his mother, was Diarmuid. He had travelled from Kilkenny, with his uncle, to work on the new chapel in the Abbey, and was staying in the shelter at the Abbey, with the rest of the masons.

It was in my mind to invite him to eat with us but we were unprepared for a guest. I took leave of him reluctantly, but before I went, he asked where he could find me again. I described the house for him.

'And what would your husband think if a strange man came to your door?'

'My husband's thoughts are on other things now, he is with his Creator.'

'I'm sorry for your loss.'

'Life is a strange son.'

'Pardon?'

'Life is strange indeed.'

I left my rainbow-hearted mason and walked, as if on a hill top, home. For the rest of the night, all my thoughts were of Diarmuid; his eyes, his hands, the way I felt when I was with him. I couldn't sleep and my mother snapped at me for tossing and turning. Since my sister joined us, my mother and I shared one bed and Eimear and Bridín shared the other. I was still awake when the cockerel crowed. And when I heard the hammering of stone from the Abbey, each stone that echoed struck a joyful note in me. Was it Diarmuid that made the rocks ring?

I didn't know it then, but that morning marked the end of a peaceful part of my life. At first the news that Geoffrey brought didn't seem so serious. The cattle had fallen dead on the land where they stood; half of the sheriff's herd had been struck down. There was often news like this, and it usually turned out to be exaggerated. The townspeople were worse than ourselves for embellishing stories.

A squawking gander announced a stranger at the door. I heard Bridín say 'Shoo,' to the bird. She was grasping the foreign language with speed and ease. And then I heard a man speaking and I knew the voice to be Diarmuid's. I hadn't mentioned him to anyone. It was my own portion of happiness and it satisfied something in me to withhold it from the others. Bridín shouted 'Roisín!' and I forgot about the dead cows and went to meet Diarmuid.

Chapter 8
Brother John
Saint John's Priory, Tristledermot, 1304 – 1311

The wild Irish say that the faeries can't cross the threshold of a monastery. For this reason, the year that the grain was bad, people came to us for flour and bread. They thought that the faeries had cursed the crop and that those who used it would waste away. They said that the flour from the monastery was free from the curse. Brendan and I were young men then. At first the crowds were small and we gave them our own supplies, and blessed the people with holy water and prayed. As the days went on, however, the numbers increased and it was beyond us to continue to provide for them.

The Prior was away at that time. When the Dean of the Priory, Brother Baptiste, tried to explain to the people that we were running out of food, they got angry and pelted him with dung. They said that we were no better than the Abbot and the monks in the Abbey and this provoked in the Dean such a response that the people were quieted for a time.

'Every one of us has taken an oath of poverty. We divide our belongings on entry to this place of God and we give all we have to the poor and sick. The rest we sustain ourselves with, in order that we can serve God. You would do well to turn to God, who has all power, and stop this talk of curses and faeries. The crop has failed because of the bad weather. If you think you would get more help in the Abbey, go there.'

The people stood facing us, and although they were silent, it felt like a protest. Silence and hunger have large voices. I could see Nuala and Brendan speaking at the back of the crowd. Brendan had grown over the summer and towered above the old woman. And then Brendan marched to where Brother Baptiste was standing. I saw him whisper to the Dean and then turn to the crowd.

'The Prior himself has poured water from the holy well into the barrel beside it and blessed it three times. He has called on Saint Mary Magdalene and Saint John the Baptist, the saints of this order, to bless your homes, yourselves and your children. This holy water and your faith will protect you from the good people. We will feed you what we can but you must be patient. We are preparing stir-about. Brother Baptiste will lead you in prayer until this is ready. Now turn your attention to your prayers.'

He strode off to the bakehouse, and although Brother Baptiste did lead the prayers, I could see that he was furious. Brendan had undermined him, in front of everyone, and he would pay for it later.

After the food was brought, Brother Baptiste ordered me to go to the town to inform the Governor that we needed the assistance of the guards. I knew it was because of what Brendan had done. He was going to punish Brendan by punishing the crowd. I asked Nuala to tell Brendan what was happening; he was giving the holy water to the people. They were carrying it in their skins and cups and any vessel that they could find. There wasn't going to be time to get to everyone.

I heard Nuala speak in her own language to the people at the door of the cookhouse and I saw the people pass her message between them. They grabbed elbows and arms and spoke in low tones and the people with children immediately moved, heading north towards the kilns, away from the town and the monastery.

I walked as slowly as I could. The distance between Saint John's and the town is slight. The guards were not at the gate and I was glad of the delay as I gained entry. I found the Governor in the courtyard beside the castle. There were soldiers arming. They sat upon heavy horses and were dressed in metal that glinted in the sun. There was excitement in the air and in the loud shouts of the soldiery. The sight was terrifying. Weapons were secured and men on foot held crossbows. There were at least twenty men, all prepared to kill. The road was empty of townspeople and doors and shutters were bolted.

I wished I had Brendan's courage as I approached the Governor. I felt as if I were demanding the slaughter of innocents.

'Brother Baptiste ordered me to let you know that the guards might be needed at the Priory.'

'We've already heard that there was trouble stirring.'

'There hasn't been any trouble, sir. The people are hungry and afraid.'

He stared at me. His face was narrow and sallow. His features and movements were sharp. There was something about him that was dagger-like.

Brother John

'You come from an order of fighting monks, young man, but I can see you are misplaced.' He smirked. 'Years ago, the monks in the Priory were magnificent knights. Make no mistake, this time the mob has asked you for the flour. If you don't show strength, next time they'll help themselves.'

He nodded to the man astride a great grey horse, who raised a staff of colours above his head. The men began to move out. The metal clanking and hooves thundering and the dust rising left me feeling powerless and alone.

I followed behind, although I wanted to run away. It was truly the first time that I had been ordered to do something that went against my will and seemed to go against God Himself. I prayed for mercy and for the protection of the people. I reassured myself that the soldiers were already on their way before my request, that I hadn't contributed to their coming. But I felt again like a coward; unwilling to fight, unwilling to pay the price that would have been asked of me had I refused my order. I knew I had made a huge mistake.

The pilgrims had dwindled in number by the time the soldiers arrived. There were some men within the walls of the Priory garden, and more straggling behind the main crowd, on the road heading north. Brendan was with the men who were standing just inside the Priory garden. His hair was wild, his face red. He looked my way and in the instant of his glance, we recognised that we were on either side of a battle. He stood with his wild friends and I was behind the soldiers.

It was in that moment too that I realised that I didn't want to fight anyone, on any side, for any reason. This, it seemed to me, is never a noble quality in a young man. But in those troubled times it was detestable. The soldiers lined the road outside the wall, and the Captain entered the Priory garden. There was a time that the grounds of the Priory ensured protection for those upon them. Since the massacre at St Mullins, however, we could no longer rely on that.

The Captain demanded to speak to the Prior. His face was dark and scowling. Brother Francis emerged from the side of the chapel and spoke to him.

'Thank you for attending to us, sir. The Prior is not within. He was called away on church business. There were people here in great numbers and it seemed that things might become difficult. But, this morning, Brother Baptiste spoke with the crowd and they moved off without complaint. I'm sorry for the trouble it has given you and your men.'

'These are not pilgrims.' The Captain looked at the men before him.

'They are here to attend Mass and receive the sacrament of Confession. Some of them are to be married on the anniversary of St John the Baptist.'

Brother Francis tried to sound convincing, but the tension was palpable. The Captain's hand was on the hilt of his sword. If he drew it, we could be sure of a fight. A shout from outside the Priory gate caught the Captain's attention and he rode out to the waiting soldiers.

A man bellowed in pain. Some soldiers had pursued the stragglers and struck them down. Three men were lying on the ground. Two no longer had life in their bodies. One was attempting to drag himself closer to one of the corpses.

I ran to the wounded man and knelt by his side. He pointed to the other man and said in his own language, 'My brother, Colm'. I caught him beneath his shoulders and dragged him towards Colm. There was blood still pouring from his brother's stomach and his entrails were spilling out with it. I absolved him of his sins and blessed him. The young man kissed his brother, and wiped his face with desperate tears. I knew the sound of a heart breaking by then. I looked away to the other body, lying on the road. Brother Francis was blessing it and Brendan was crying. The man was known to him.

We tended to the bodies and then brought the wounded man to the hospital. We passed a large crowd of people coming from the cloister. Brother Francis had hidden them when he'd heard that the soldiers were coming. It was a dark day for all of us.

Brendan left the Priory that very night and I lost my dearest friend and any peace I'd known until then. I was haunted by restlessness, by my own cowardice and by the evil deeds of men. Brendan said that the Nolan clan in Loughlin was raising a force of fighting men and it was his intention to join them. He said he was sick of being pushed around by mercenaries and foreigners, that the war between our people was getting worse. 'I have to go where I'm needed most,' he said.

'God bless you and keep you safe, brother. I won't forget you in my prayers. You will be a warrior like the great Finn Mac Cumhail,' I said.

Even this didn't make him smile.

I heard afterwards that when Brother Francis had taken the people into the Priory, some of the men had decided to place themselves within sight of the soldiers, to distract them. The young man who died had willingly put himself between the soldiers and the people, in the hope that the others might live.

'The deeds of that young man were like those of the Fianna, I was of no use to the people at all.'

Brendan walked away from the Priory and the religious life. The life we'd known together ended that day.

Brendan returned to his own people and I determined to travel. Our lives are not pre-ordained, Brother Francis said. We always have the freedom to choose the path to Our Lord and there's always hope of salvation.

There's so much destruction, killing and evil in the hearts of men and so much sadness and suffering. Perhaps if I followed in the footsteps of Jesus and found the Holy Land, Our Lord might save me from cowardice, might bestow on me the peace of the old pilgrim monk I had met that day.

I determined to take with me parchment and the tools of the scribe and write my own words. The wild Irish and the Saxons have their stories. I wanted to make a record of my tales and those I might find along my travels.

Brother Francis said that he would be sorry to see me leave. He relied on me but he said that, if I must leave, I should go to one of the French Monasteries, where I would be welcomed. Without coin I would have to beg my sustenance and passage, but this did not deter me. It would keep me in the company of the poor and this was what I wanted.

Chapter 9
Rose
Tristledermot, 1324

When the early autumn sun touched the green glass of the huge Abbey windows, it cast a light over the whole town. The morning glow was like an invitation to pray. It was the eve of the feast of Saint James, a martyr who was revered in the town. The two religious houses, usually at odds about which saints were most worthy of celebrating, were both in agreement about Saint James. He was a brother of Saint John the Evangelist and known affectionately by the townspeople, along with Saint John, as 'one of the sons of thunder.'

The first apples and berries were picked. In the sheltered green ground of the Governor, all manner of early fruits thrived. The keeper of the Governor's lands, Giuseppe the Grower, was a man of dark skin and strange tongue. He was different to everyone in the town and beyond. He brought with him knowledge of plants that, most thought, was divinely given. He could manipulate nature to grow out of season and could create strong seedlings in years of drought or rain.

Along the town road, the places of the tanners, weavers, smiths, cobblers, candlemakers, tailors and carpenters were all closed early. The butcher and baker provided breaded meat to the Abbey and it would be given to the people after the Mass that evening, along with the harvested fruits.

Rose

The Abbey was one of the great churches and was attended regularly by the wealthy of the town. It was a place where indulgences could be bought and where regular donations would ensure the good status of the donor. On feast days, the seating arrangements within the church were related to the importance of the members of the congregation. The wealthiest were placed nearest to the altar, close to where the Governor had his own seat. The poor, the wild Irish and ordinary women without husbands stood at the back near the shrine. In the years of famine and sickness, the Abbey prospered more than in years of plenty.

Diarmuid finished his work early on the eve of the feast of Saint James. The monks wished for quietness in order to prepare themselves for their day of prayer. I tried to hide my delight in seeing him, knowing my mother was watching.

'The child is yours?' he asked.

'She's my sister's daughter. I have no children.'

'Yet,' he said. 'You have none yet.'

I'm sure I blushed at his words. My sister came from the miller's house and seeing us, joined me.

'This is Bridín's mother now – Eimear,' I said.

'Your daughter is beautiful, like her mother,' said Diarmuid.

A jealous pain stuck itself in my heart. It was only pleasant talk, the kind we all make and the force of my jealousy surprised me. Eimear wasn't sure what he meant, but smiled and then reddened, as their eyes met. This man must have the same power over all women. I was foolish

1324

to think I was the only one who felt drawn to him. I made an excuse to go into our dwelling and didn't invite him within. He said he was going to *The Garter Inn* and would see us the following day at Mass.

My mother was plucking a bird and complaining about the woman who had come to kill it.

'I gave her coin and she took it. I thought she was skilled in the killing of poultry but, long after she'd gone, this poor creature and another hen could be heard screeching. I'll never employ her again and I've a good mind to demand compensation for her shabby work. I had to wring their necks myself. The poor things, killed twice over.'

Eimear was staring through the open door to where Diarmuid had stood. She was touching the table top and humming. Her fair hair was drawn into a high plait and her neck was still carrying the burnt scars from the heat of the fire that had destroyed our clan. She was lovely. Her face had been sad for so long that despite myself, I was glad to see some life in her eyes.

'Who was the man at the gate?' asked my mother.

Eimear looked to me. I was about to speak when Bridín spoke.

'That's Diarmuid. He called to find our Roisín,'

'Ah, Diarmuid na mban,' my mother said.

Eimear smiled broadly.

'Diarmuid of the women,' Bridín translated, her new game.

'You didn't invite him in?' my mother said.

'He's just someone I met at the fair yesterday. He helped with the carrying of the goods as far as the square. He's a mason from Kilkenny.'

Rose

'A soft man of stone,' said my mother. She too was watching Eimear smile.

'How is Ava?'

'The baby hasn't turned yet, but any day now will see her labour begin.'

'And will you deliver it?'

'I will, please God,' said Eimear.

We had many reasons for prayer. Try as I might, I could not stop thinking of the mason.

It was just before the curfew sounded that Diarmuid came to our door again. His knocking was urgent and startled us. He was beer-breathed and at first I thought he was drunk.

'The cattle are dying all over the land, I've heard it myself from the Earl's men. They say the Earl has lost three quarters of his whole herd. They dropped dead where they stood. The pastures are heavy with dead stock. Make your food stores secure, there'll be trouble.'

My mother spoke calmly, introduced herself and offered Diarmuid some ale. She reassured him, described the famine that she'd survived, and reminded him that a cattle plague went through the land some years before. Diarmuid drank, but still he seemed shaken.

'That's not all. My uncle has just returned from Kilkenny and brought back with him an account of the flogging of Petronella de Midia. He saw it with his own eyes.'

We'd heard about the witch in Kilkenny. Who hadn't? The new clergy held opinions on matters of which they knew little. But this was

1324

different, Diarmuid said. This would be a trial held in a court of law and there were accusations of sexual relations with demons and sacrifices to the devil. The woman was known to his family.

'The bastard bishop, Ledrede, has had her publicly flogged and imprisoned and they say she'll be burnt alive. I can't repeat what my uncle said about it.' He glanced at Bridín and then continued.

'She's no more a witch than I am. Ledrede has an axe to grind with Alice Kytler, who wormed her way out as the wealthy often do, leaving her poor servant, that innocent, to suffer in her stead.'

The news was disturbing but the recent merciless burning and murdering of our own people by the Bishop's men was still with us and left us little room for sympathy.

We talked of other matters and Bridín sang her latest song about the cess pit where the guards gathered in the mornings. Diarmuid's mood lightened a little. I played my flute, an old air to start with, and then a livelier one.

'The cess pit or the town guards are no company for a little girl, Bridín. Stay away from there. Come on, Diarmuid, up you get. I'm not too old to do a turn of the floor.'

My mother held her hand out to our guest. They danced and he was graceful on his feet. My mother looked younger when she moved to music. It was as if she stepped into the child she once was. I repeated the tune and they spun around the hearth. When I finished, my mother was out of breath and Diarmuid was smiling.

Eimear left to attend to Ava again. Diarmuid's eyes followed her to the door; a sharp twist of the blade of jealousy injured me again. I tried to hide it, but my mother saw things clearly. There was no place unseen in our dwelling, not even in the secret places of the heart.

The cattle plague was worse than we could ever have imagined. Within days any stock that had been within the town was dead, as was most of what lay beyond. In some areas every single cow and bull went the same way. The rare cow left standing refused to give milk, and there was none who blamed her. All other stock seemed unaffected and the goats that the Governor had brought into the town the previous year proved to be our saviours. The billy goats were put to work increasing the numbers of their breed and the price of goats' milk went up.

There was pork and veal to be had along with other meats, but the prices were beyond most people. Animal feed was cheap and we stored as much of it as we could in our outbuilding. We'd have need of the rat catcher that year. The smell from the dead beasts was heavy in the air. It worked through our clothing and onto our skin. The cloths we were making garments of held the stench and we burned thyme and rosemary to try to cover the smell by day, and by night we doused them in rose water.

The night guards reported packs of wolves scavenging and wild Irish cutting up chunks of beef to carry away. Most of us were afraid to eat the meat of the dead beasts. The physician had said that the disease might infect those who consumed it and again there were rumours of witchcraft.

1324

Before the month was out, the Governor ordered that every man be employed in burying the animals. Unsuccessful attempts had been made to burn them. Even Geoffrey the miller was obliged to spend seven days labouring in this way. It was a gruesome task. The weight of the beasts made the transporting of them difficult. Huge holes were dug all over the land, close to where the animals lay. The butcher had to carve up the creatures who were hard to reach, and for the others the masons created a lifting system with wood, ropes and wheels. The cattle were placed upon carts that strained the horses to move. When they were carried to the pits, it took five men to push a beast in.

Stephen, the gravedigger, was to oversee the interment of the cows. A man of low standing, but with a good eye for opportunity, demanded a price from Stephen for the use of his horses and cart. For his cheek, the Governor had the man whipped and tied for a day outside the parliament house. There was to be no profiting on the disposal of cattle, he said.

The men were exhausted at the end of their days. The Governor ordered all other people, except for those engaged in the essential work of providing food, to attend to the agriculture of the crops and other animals. Giuseppe the Grower oversaw the tending of vegetables and grain and it was on us to follow his every back-breaking instruction. My mother and Bridín were slow for different reasons. Bridín was not yet strong and my mother's bones were weakened by her years. They were tasked to weed and water.

Eimear and I worked alongside the itinerant reapers and put

ourselves into the work with all our might. We cut corn, picked cabbage and kale and used scythes to mow hay. It was painful work. At the end of every long day, the hoteliers in *The Garter Inn* filled our bowls with mutton broth, chicken soup, jugged rabbit or croustades of fish; any dish that would go far enough to feed the whole town. Diarmuid and his father would meet with us there. Even though there was worry about raids and we were all tired, the mood of the people as we ate the evening meal was jubilant. Day by day we were surviving the catastrophe together.

Towards the end of that time, after most of the cattle were buried or burned, there was a celebration at Michaelmas to mark the end of the dreadful plague. We were all glad to be alive but there was also a lot to grieve. There would be no cattle hides to ship abroad that year and no beef. There would be no milk or cream to make cheese or butter, an unnatural absence from our table. The tanners and shoemakers were sullen, as were the agriculturists, who complained that there would be a dearth of manure for the land and no market for the hay or feed. A hard winter looked certain.

The clergy gave fish and oysters to the town, along with bread, cooked apples and ale. Mass was attended and I offered my prayers to Saint Brighid for the grace to live to see another spring. Later, as the evening sun sank behind the far hills, Diarmuid found me by the fire, listening to the music of the Irish who were lilting. Their voices followed a light tune, full of life, a dance that people loved to hear.

1324

'It's your music again, Rose. Do you dance like your mother?'

'She is a beautiful dancer. I have my father's airy tunes but his heavy feet.'

'The night I heard you play your flute, when you played the slow tune, I heard another flute playing with you. How did you do that?'

'The second piper was not my doing. It is impossible to play two flutes.'

'What was it then?' He grabbed my shoulders and then tickled my ribs. 'Was it faery music I heard?'

I laughed and ducked away from him.

'I can't say what you heard, your ears are not mine. Perhaps you should ask them?'

I leaned towards him and spoke into his ear. 'Are the Sídhe playing music within your head, mason?'

Diarmuid smiled and faced me. His eyes were amber in the fire light and his hair glowed as deep as the autumn leaves. I longed for his hands to touch my arms again. My pulse raced in his presence. His lips were close to mine and he didn't pull away. 'O Rose, you are beautiful!' I put my hand upon his and my skin and heart sang for him. He took my wrist and every move of his fingers was like a dance. We walked through the town, to the outbuildings at the back of the castle, where the abundant hay was stored. I followed him as if under a spell. I had no care of who might see us. He removed his cloak and laid it on the floor.

'Lie with me, Rose,' he said and I lay on his thick woollen cloak. The hay beneath made a soft bed. He kissed my ready lips and my soul

Rose

was lifted to a place beyond the town, the land, into the night sky. His mouth spoke to my neck, my breasts, my waiting bush. I felt the shape of his strength in his arms, his chest and his legs and I touched the softness of his skin, of his loving body. His manhood was as hard as the stones he chiselled. He touched me and my voice cried out with pleasure. He moved himself on my wet bush until I felt a surge that was like a furnace in my very being, and then he entered me and together we soared amongst the heavens.

When we were spent, we fell asleep, and there we remained until the sounds of the town disturbed us early the following morning. When I returned home, Bridín was alone in her cot. There was nobody else within. Ava was in labour, she said, since the night before and the others were with her. I lay beside Bridín, my limbs aching, and fell into a deep sleep.

'So, you are back with us,' a voice snapped.

I opened my eyes to see my mother and then felt a sharp clip on my ear.

'Where did you go so late?' she said.

I ignored her. Perhaps she didn't know how late it had been.

'Has Ava had the child?' I asked.

'She is still in labour. Your sister's hands are blessed by God. She said the baby had been in a bad position and she has spent the night coaxing it to turn.

'And how is Ava?'

1324

'She's exhausted, but in good spirits,'

Everyone knows the dangers of childbirth. So many women take their last breath as their infant takes its first and so many babies fall into the eternal sleep before their eyes open. It can be the cruellest time in a woman's life. With difficulty I rose from the bed. My mother, who sees all, left the room.

I was sure that Diarmuid loved me. The way we had been together was still tender and warm in my heart, but happiness is a fool's sauce. I didn't see Diarmuid for the rest of the day. Ava had a long labour and her wailing could be heard through the town. I was sure it was a bad birth and then, as the evening darkened again, I heard the small and distinct noise of a new born. It was accompanied by the church bell ringing. It was as if the whole town sighed with relief. When we went to see the baby, Eimear was holding it, and talking softly. It was a scene of divine beauty.

I didn't see Diarmuid for days, but the masons could be heard working at the other side of the wall. The more time passed, the more each note, hammered on the stone, wounded me. I inquired of Stephen if he'd heard of any accidents at the Abbey, but he said there were none. Why did Diarmuid absent himself? The ways of men are strange.

A play in the town brought everybody out. It was a warm day in late autumn, the feast of Saint Francis. The play was about the life of the saint; his life of sin, his imprisonment and his conversion. The players stood high on the Governor's cart for all to see. They began their story at the north gate and finished at the south gate, the crowd moving along with them. Although the crowd was jovial and raucous, as they saw Francis boast of his conquests of having one woman after the next, I was desolate. And when Francis stripped himself naked, returning his clothes to the bishop, the crowd cheered and I could stand it no longer. I ran home, the din following me.

Eimear was the first home after me.

'Where did you get to? The play was entertaining.'

'I was tired and cold.'

'And you missed Diarmuid's uncle.'

I paid attention to her then, wondering if she knew what had happened between Diarmuid and me. I wanted to know if his uncle had said where Diarmuid had gone, but couldn't ask her. When we were children, we used to play a game called 'find'. One of us would hide something and the other had to find it. It was a game that could take days.

'Diarmuid's a fine looking man. Every girl in the town notices him. You must surely be of the same mind,' said Eimear.

My legs went heavy and I felt sick.

'He's a good man,' I said.

'He is. He'd make a fine brother-in-law for you!'

She was smiling brightly and her eyes were full of life and hope. I couldn't help myself from saying, 'But can you be sure he'd make a good husband?' It was as if I had thrown damp sods on her joy.

'You're never happy with people. They are never good enough for

1324

you,' she barked. 'You left your own kind behind, and now you're miserable because you're without your husband and he left you no children. You've more wealth than I've ever seen and still it's not enough for you.'

'You forget, I left the clan because my husband died. I couldn't look at the place without him. Well, now I've buried two husbands, does that satisfy you? Did I deserve that?'

Her anger was up, and she said things that I wish she hadn't, and I returned her slights with greater insults. Eimear flung a bowl that caught the side of my head. It shattered on the flags.

'What the devil is going on?'

My mother stood between us.

'Put yourselves together. You don't have to tell me what this is about. There's a pair of you in it.'

Jealousy and temper sent me out of the dwelling. The dark outline of the Abbey rose like a headless creature. I rushed to the west gate where the guard told me that the curfew was in place and I had no right to be abroad.

'I have business with St John's that can't wait.'

'Then you want the north gate, Weaver.'

'It's a dressmaker I am, and I want to leave by this gate.'

He opened the gate and I raced towards the Priory lights.

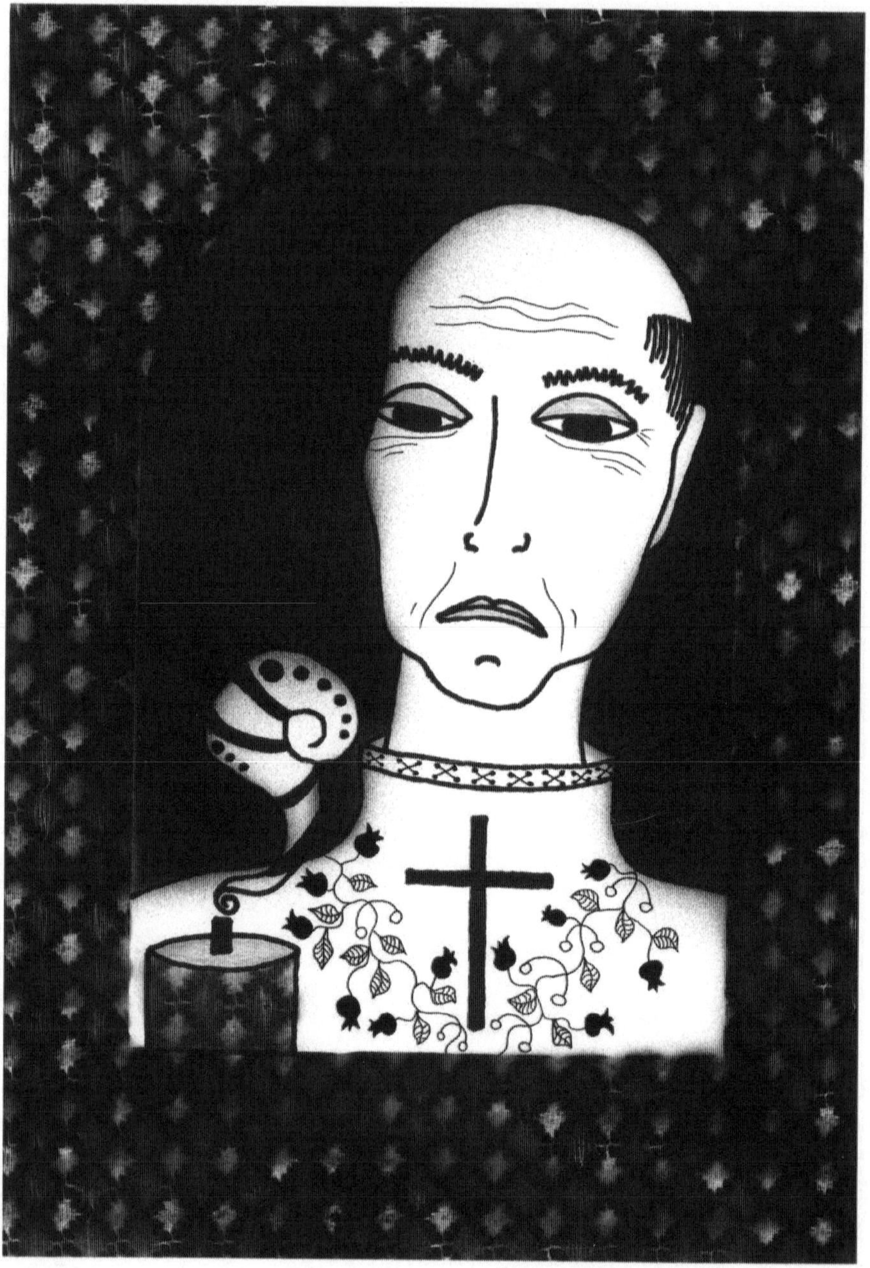

Chapter 10
Brother John
Bristowe, England, 1311

No one boards a vessel without fears but, more than ever before in my life, my faith was absolute. Whatever my Creator had designed for me, I was willing to complete. If the ship went down, I would meet Him with a good heart. My reliance on Our Lord and Saint John gave me a feeling of tremendous joy. I watched all around me as if viewing my last sights. The horses and asses hauling goods; the crooked traders shouting to sell wares not permitted in the markets; the women standing ready for the coin of a mariner; the men loading and unloading; boats of different sizes coming and going, magnificent sails pulled upwards as the boats got past the throng. It was a feast for the senses like none I'd seen before. If it was to be my last view, I was well satisfied. I wasn't to know that the port I would enter was going to be thrice the size of the one I was leaving.

On board I found a space on the deck and was advised to tie myself to a stay next to me. The boat was stout and broad, with a huge sail that stretched upwards so high that the mariner in the crow's nest almost vanished from my sight as he ascended.

'Try to avoid anyone looking green; spew sticks and stinks.' A seaman offered me a rope. The boat was packed with wool. There were few passengers: another monk, a family, some merchants, slaves, and men to tend to both the shackled animals and people on board. Avery would have loved this voyage.

When the shout went up that we were nearing the port of Bristowe, I was tired and wet but full of hope. The seaman was right about the spew and I wanted to find a place to wash and steady myself again. The sea moves the river's sands in the bay outside the port of Bristowe and we had to wait some time before the boat could dock. The animals stamped with impatience and a small child among the slaves complained. One of the men raised a rod and beat both the mother and the child, shouting at them as he did this.

'You better all shut up and make yourselves agreeable, or I'll sell you to the devil himself when we get to market.'

The Crouched Friars, my own order, were known for our position on slavery. We followed the church teachings and new church laws and tried to insist that others did the same. Having survived the passage, my conviction was stronger than ever. I reminded myself that I was on this boat because of my cowardice, and that I had vowed to do as my Maker asked of me. I got to my feet.

'No one but God can possess the soul of a man, woman or child.'

I looked to the slaves, six men, six women and the child, and stated, 'St Mathew said *do not fear those who kill the body but cannot kill the soul.*'

I turned towards the man whose hand was clutching the stick and

1311

continued, '*Rather fear Him who can destroy both soul and body in hell.*'

The man struck the mother of the child again.

'Your holy books are better preached in Latin. Follow their instruction yourselves before you think of teaching anyone else.'

I ignored his comments, astute as they were, and prayed for the protection of Saint John. I remembered every word that I had copied of his gospel and every feature of his face, like that of a well-known friend which was etched on my soul.

'*And not be like Cain, who was of the Evil One and murdered his brother. And why did he murder him? Because his own deeds were evil and his brother's righteous.*'

The man paused, and although the bones in his hands were white where they grasped the rod, he stopped beating the slaves. The mariners were looking on.

'Even you are called by Our Lord; even you can be redeemed in Him.'

'Get out of my sight, Priest, before I batter you!'

The boat began to sway again and I was compelled to run to the side and retch. The ship travelled at great speed on currents into the port of Bristowe. There was no more conflict until long after we docked.

The port was large beyond belief and the town was teeming with people, some with strangely hued skin. I had little coin, but in my satchel I had

Brother John

parchment and ink. I was as happy as I'd ever felt, but tired. The evening drew in, and with it the town was changing. Buildings lit up as far as the eye could see. People were making merry in the inns, and women were walking along the streets in pairs. There was an air of menace in the shadows, but compared to the particular sense of danger before a raid, it was a small thing. The walls of the town must have been miles long and a splendid castle stood behind still more walls. Although there was a large church near the castle, it was the shelter of somewhere less elaborate that I sought. A church bell nudged me to prayer and I took it as a sign that my Lord and Saint John were calling to me.

I wandered in the direction of the sound. Rows of large dwellings, with green ground between them and before them, stood along wide roads. Through doorways, people could be seen talking, dining, moving. Smoke billowed from high chimneys. I heard my own language and that of the Saxons spoken. I passed several churches and asked the way to the monastery, for I was sure it was the bell of a monastery I could hear.

'There's more than one monastery but you're best to go to the Priory of Saint James' beyond the town walls. You will see it from the north gate.'

It wasn't long before I found the Priory and there requested refuge.

Everything in the town, even its people, was larger than home. Saint James' was the size of a small town and the Benedictine monks that lived there were many in number. I was welcomed as a brother. The Crouched Friars and Benedictines were known to be hospitallers, but they lived by different rules. This didn't seem to perturb my host. When

1311

I said I was a scribe, I was invited to the library, the room of books. Its shelves were full of bibles and psalters and uncommon copies of poetry. More books than I had ever seen. Brother Robert was a scribe too; he was older than me and seemed happy with my enthusiasm for words.

'In this town, the wealthy have books they never read. They order them for show.'

'What kinds of books do they like to show?' I asked.

'Psalters, prayer books, poetry and most have bibles. They like decorative work. Do you draw as well as write?'

I did, I told him, and he said I should stay a while and help him; the wealthy townspeople had more silver to spend on books than he could supply. And how could I, a brother of a different order, remain with him? I asked. I was on my way to our monastery in France. People on pilgrimage often stay, he told me. If I were a good scribe, the Priory would welcome the help. He had too much to do, teaching bad students to write. I took it as a sign from Saint John and decided to stay for a short time. I could be happy drawing and writing and hoped Brother Robert would be pleased by my work.

For days I worked, copying in the scriptorium, before venturing beyond the Priory walls again. I was one of fifty scribes. I was surprised to see that half of the scribes were lay men. In the Priory at home, this was unheard of, although I had often wondered why. I was to learn afterwards that most of the lay men did not read, and theirs was the task of copying simple words. Those skilled in the art of illumination were

Brother John

scarce, and it was for this that I was employed. The materials we used were brought into the room by those whose task it was to make the ink and procure parchment. On the first day, I noticed a stack of gold leaf and an abundance of candles and quills. The colours of the inks were spectacular; vermillion from Spain, yellows from Asia and more orange lead, minium, than I'd ever seen.

The first book that was given to me was *The Hours of the Virgin*, a book of prayers that I knew by heart. We were to illuminate a full page, with a drawing from the life of Mary before each division. We would also copy the calendar, pictures and prayers from the book. This was the most elaborate copy that I'd ever seen. It was the usual practice to illuminate the first letter of the divisions. The devotion to, and creation of, a whole page of artistry was lavish beyond measure in a common prayer book. The calendar was slightly different from the one I knew. There were feast days of saints that I'd never heard of and I saw the other scribes drawing images of people and kings that were of a different fashion to my own. Richard the Lionheart was one such person. The decorative work of the pages was not as intricate as the kind I was used to, and so I worked quickly.

My desk was near one of the many pale glass windows in the scriptorium and, as light faded, I prepared to finish the day's work. A servant entered and lit so many candles that it was as bright as day, save for the shadow of my hand.

I looked at the other scribes, their backs twisted and hunched. In the Priory in Tristledermot, we used candles in the winter but when the day

1311

was long, it was considered enough to use the light given by Our Lord and retire when night fell. I noticed a monk and a lay man at the front of the room, communicating by use of their hands. Something amused them, and their shaking shoulders betrayed their laughter. The chief draughtsman, who had been busy correcting the work of a lay man, saw their movements, stormed down to them, caught their ears and marched them outside. A thin sheet of gold leaf wafted upwards in the breeze in their wake and a lay man desperately tried to rescue it, without tearing the delicate sheet.

Some days later, my body inhibited by pain, I asked Brother Robert for permission to leave the Priory. I hadn't seen him since the day I'd arrived. I found him in the library, a servant pouring wine for him. Around his neck was a thick gold chain that was visible under his garments. He seemed pleased to see me and gladly gave me leave to walk abroad. He drew coin from a purse.

'Take this, young monk, for the toll bridge and some extra. You will have plenty of need for it in the town. Be back for evening prayers.'

It was a sunny autumn day. A strong wind cleared the air and I made towards the town. The land on either side of the road was marshy. I paid the toll at Frome Gate and crossed the river. Painted carts carried finely dressed women and men and others strolled with pride in costly clothes and shoes. The markets were open in buildings along the road leading to the quay. Casks of wine and barrels of ale were to be seen, and the wool market was overrun with merchants shouting and bargaining. The corn market had a long row of carts harnessed to horses and oxen, waiting patiently for their loads. The clouds of dust and chaff, rising from the area, reminded me of the harvest at home. Along the road, and at the market, were several wells where people filled pails, and animals drank from full troughs. Stalls of cooks stood together, stewing meats in large cauldrons and roasting breaded dishes over the fires for passers-by. Beneath their feet cats scavenged, while occasionally, a brave rat or mouse could be seen carrying off a morsel. It seemed to me that there was such abundance in this town that the people didn't know real need.

The smells of the meat and fish markets lingered close to the quay, where they were situated, and every kind of merchandise could be seen. Bags of spices and strange fare were displayed. My head was dizzy, gazing at one wonder after the next, and the port offered no rest. The river was full of ships. A cog, with lowered sails, was just docking. Ropes were thrown to waiting men, who tied them fast, and great planks were pushed out to enable the people to land. Immediately the activity around the ship became frantic, as wool and other goods were unloaded. I heard Irish spoken and many other tongues too.

'Clear out of the way, Monk.' A seaman was throwing sacks from the deck into a heap beside me. I sat away from the boats and watched instead the work and busyness, longing again to board a vessel and sail to another unknown land.

'Are you a fighting monk?'

A woman had noticed the red cross of my vestments. Many orders wore the cross, including the Templars.

'No, it's the cross of an Order of Hospitallers, the Crouched Friars.'

1311

She was green-eyed and sallow-skinned, with brown hair that shone in the sun. She wore an apron of a working woman and spoke Saxon with a peculiar accent.

'When did you arrive?' she asked.

I told her of my journey and said I was a scribe staying in Saint James'.

'Plenty of silver in the pockets of the monks in the Priory.'

'It seems all in this town have plenty.'

'Not everything is as it seems. The poor are on the far side of the town, away from the markets and the Exchange. The Earl doesn't want the pitiable poor to be the first things visitors see when they arrive in the city.'

'You have several churches here. The people must be devout to need so many.'

She threw her head upwards and laughed.

'You are new to the ways of the town, young monk. The people here have a greater need than most for prayer, but few spend time in churches.'

She said her name was Agnes, that her father was a blacksmith and her mother had been a fish seller. When her mother died, Agnes took up her place at the market, but then traded her fish licence for that of a dyer.

'Since the wool market became so busy, the need for dyers grew and I learned the trade with speed.'

It was then that I noticed her hands were darkly stained. They were small and the dark stains, which reached to her elbows, were like a pair of dainty silk gloves.

'Have you idle time, Friar? Can a young woman guide you from gate to gate?'

I turned by habit to ask another man whether I should walk in a strange town with a girl, but of course I was unaccompanied. I had never been alone with a young woman. Brendan used to boast about his evenings at *The Garter Inn,* but I never joined him there. Many monks and priests kept company with women. Although I had thought the cobbler's daughter very beautiful, I had never found the courage to speak with her, even before I took my final vows. Martin, my fellow scribe, frequently watched the girls that were sent from Grane to nurse the lepers and the sick, and the other boys used to go to great lengths to speak with the same girls, but I was nervous of women. Brother Francis always said that unless a man was set on marrying, he should stay away from them. Some of the boys were as attached to each other as others were to women. I had the same desires as other men. Many nights my seed spilled during my sleep or with the help of movements of my hands. Brother Francis told me this was the way a man consoled his body for the absence of a wife.

In that moment I would have gone to the ends of the earth with Agnes, had she asked. She said she could take but a short time from her work and that I would have to be quick of step. We passed a steep stairway that led to the river Frome, where washer women were scrubbing clothing. Agnes's speech was fast and there were many times

1311

I missed what she said, but the sound of her voice was enough to keep me trotting after her. The stench of human waste thickened as we walked. In Saint James' the latrine was placed directly over a running stream which, I was told, flowed into the Avon river. It was as if all the shit from this side of the town gathered at this place and flowed nowhere.

A small boy, barefooted and dirty, held his hand out to me. Agnes gave him a piece of bread from her apron, scolded him and sent him away.

'The parish gives them poor relief to stop them begging. The council would punish him if they found out. These aren't the worst of them,'

Agnes led me to a small church, through to a courtyard, where two guards stood.

'This is Blindgate. When the city is quiet the church is open; when there's trouble all the gates are shut fast.'

The guards nodded at us.

'Your rig-out allows you to travel wherever you want, Friar,' said Agnes.

We continued through the hidden gate. The dwellings were similar to those beyond the gates at home, as if all the poor were of one family, but the number of poor was so much greater here. People were thin and scantily clad, some pushing small carts of what looked like kitchen waste. They paid us no heed.

'Do you have a name?' she asked.

'Fabien.'

'Fabien, bean grower,' she said smiling. When she smiled it was as if the day were suddenly illuminated by the Lord. I hadn't said my real name in years.

We came upon a stinking pile of discarded slops – the refuse of the town. Agnes explained that the council ordered it to be deposited outside the walls. The heap had outgrown the pit. Small children and women were picking through the newly dropped loads and selecting carrot ends and other scraps. Rats were their foraging companions. Overhead, the hawks seemed sure of a good meal.

The place of the paupers saddened me. Beyond this place, at the great road into the town, knights rode in droves upon heavy horses and large companies of carts and people moved in opposite directions. We turned back to Blindgate.

'And that is the town of Bristowe, Fabien, I hope to see you on the quays again soon. Look for me in the Dyers' Hall.'

She waved a delicate hand and then quickly covered it again. I said a reluctant farewell to Agnes and retreated to St James'.

It was as if all I had known of the world until that moment was insignificant. I was a single man among legions. I had naïvely thought that I might bring God's message to the suffering. But there were so many, I would never be heard, and the suffering had more need of food than prayers. I had entered the Priory in Tristledermot as a child and I was still a child on leaving.

I had no appetite for the meal that evening. Brother Robert was in the

1311

library, where it seemed he spent most of his time.

'How goes it in the town, young John?'

I told him of the people I'd seen. He said that the ways of God were a mystery to all of us. He said my work as a scribe was very fine and that, if I stayed a while, it would serve God's work. I was defeated by the day. My ambition to serve the poor on this earth far exceeded my ability. At prayer I listened for the voice of Saint John, but couldn't hear him. The square chapel in Saint James' churchyard was full of strange images; the world here was painted differently. When I retired that night, thoughts of Agnes lifted my spirits, but I had lost my direction. Without Brother Francis to guide me, I felt alone and sure I had been mistaken in leaving all that was familiar. Confronting the slave merchant had been a good beginning, but the fear that had been hidden during the encounter returned now. Courage is a hard won prize. I lay awake, my heart pounding in the cage of my chest. I was glad of the bed beneath me, but unsure of the price it would cost.

A long week passed before I next met Agnes. Brother Robert gave me leave and coin, more than I'd ever held before. I refused it at first but he said it was a small token for my work, that the lady who'd purchased the book was wealthy and wanted to reward the draughtsman. In Saint Johns' at home, no monk had possessions. All was shared for the poor and shared for the common good. This order behaved in a different way and, not willing to offend my host, I took my payment.

I saw two women at the Priory gate. An autumn chill was in the evening air although the light was still full on the horizon. The women wore their hair high and on their heads sparkled jewels, so that when the sun was reflected, they dazzled.

'Are you on your way out or in?' one woman asked.

'I'm leaving. Can I be of assistance?'

They giggled at this.

'We won't demand a payment for looking, but if you'd like to trade with us, we will give you a good deal.'

I looked to the ground, realising that their wares were their bodies.

'Where are you from, young monk?'

'Ireland, across the sea.'

'We know where the land is. We have a street named after you.'

'After my name? Brother John?'

'Irishmead Street, duck-head. Have you seen it yet? It's close to Grope Alley.'

I said no and they chuckled. I tried to move past them, but the one closest to me caught my arm.

'If you dine with the devil, young sir, then you'll need a good long spoon!'

The chill of the air entered my bones. I wanted to ask if she was speaking of Brother Robert, but I inquired instead as to which monk they intended to see.

'Not one, but two, sir, and they pay well for our silence.'

I continued to the bridge, their words hanging on my shoulders.

1311

Agnes was outside the Dyers' Hall with two small children, her brother and sister. She was even lovelier than I had remembered. I prayed under my breath to Saint John, that my will would become the instrument of his. Agnes sent the children home.

'We will sit by the Green, near the great well,' she said.

The bells marked the hours. We sat and talked into the night.

'You are as full of chatter as a magpie,' she said. I told her as much about myself as I knew and she in turn spoke of her mother's death, of her brother and sister and how much she'd hated the fish market. She said that being born into a trade was a gift and a curse. She couldn't take on the trade of her father; women were forbidden in the forge. Her neighbour took her on as a fishmonger and then the woman's husband tried to have his way with her.

'Too much ale and wine stir up lechery and drunkenness and lead to wickedness. My neighbour put the blame on me and asked the fishermen to stop selling to me. My father went to the council and begged to trade the licence for another one. A man there took pity on him, for he knew my mother's family, and arranged an apprenticeship with a dyer. Now my hands are tainted blue and my reputation is tainted along with them.'

'Your hands are beautiful, Agnes.'

I wanted to touch her hands and arms. It came into my mind that I wanted to kiss them. I felt a rush of lust, like a bolt of thunder through my body. My face was hot despite the cold. Agnes brushed her fingertips over my hands, and my prick hardened. She edged closer and kissed my cheek; her lips like warm wishes talked to my heart. I had never desired communion so completely with another person until then.

She pulled away, stood and straightened her garments.

'My father will be wondering where I am. It's long past a respectable hour and you will be chastised for consorting with a woman.'

'I don't think anyone would notice and, as it so happens, the monks in Saint James' have relations with women.'

As soon as I said that I regretted it.

'Oh and you are just doing as the rest of them? You should be so fortunate as to have relations with a woman like me, Fabien! I thought you were of a different kind.'

She was annoyed with me and I couldn't think of what to say. A group of men could be heard singing a sea shanty in a nearby tavern. It was as if the ground underneath me was moving, like the shifting sands of the harbour. I knew only about how to live in the shelter of a monastery. I knew the prayers which marked each day and the feast days that kept time with the year. I could repeat the words of the psalms and gospels and create drawings that were so beautiful that the presence of God could be felt in them. Yet, now I felt utterly stupid. I had no business with a woman.

The Priory was a place that Brother Francis would have despised. Silence was not observed in any place. The stores were overflowing and the unfree people, who worked in the kitchen and on the land, were

1311

treated badly. The senior monks lived separately to the rest of us and there was gold and silver everywhere. I had imagined that, without the threat of raids and war, life would have been peaceful, but peace was the property of the wealthy, at the cost of the poor. The faces of the people beyond the walls were still with me. It was as if I were being tested by Our Lord. To leave demanded more courage than I had and I was afraid. I prayed to Saint John for help and thought of my mother, who must by now be with him.

An errand sent me to the town soon again. I looked for Agnes on the quay, but could not find her. Neither was she in the Dyers' Hall, but a man there told me that she was at a burial.

'Whose?' I asked.

'Her little sister, Bracy, lost her life in a well, and is this day being buried alongside her mother.'

The man's tears ran down his face; his arms were red with stains and heat. I thought of the child that had been so happy to meet me, her carefree laughter gone now from this world. The sands beneath me were moving again. O God, whose mercy knows no bounds, bless Bracy and all she has left behind. I thanked the man and blessed him. He made the sign of the cross and, with a falling heart, I went to Agnes's dwelling.

I recognised the house by the crowd of dyers and smiths coming from it. Agnes was among them, her face pale.

'I heard of Bracy's death.'

She nodded and stared at me. The life in her swollen eyes was dull.

Brother John

There was nothing I could say.

'Thank you for coming. I'm going back to work. There's nothing more I can do for her.'

I remembered what Brother Francis used to say at such times and thought of the silver in my purse. I pressed it into her palm.

'I have no use for this coin. The death of a child is an unexpected burden, in ways I can't imagine. Please take it.'

She tried to refuse, but hadn't the strength, and nodded again instead. I felt lighter in spirits as I left her, despite the desolate loss. She had helped me far more than I had helped her. The vows I'd taken were burning in my heart again. Bracy's death would not be in vain. I would not store wealth, but would give instead to the needy and put my faith in God.

Brother Robert heard my confession. I confessed to the sins of lust and greed. He gave absolution and penance. Outside the chapel, he said that a man's passions were given by God, that the life of a good draughtsman like me could be a comfortable one. I wasn't listening to his smooth words any longer. Reason has rule over passion, I told him. He laughed uproariously at this. I told him that my ambition was to help the suffering and speak the Word of God. His face and voice changed like a sudden blast of cold wind.

'If you preach in this town, with no authority from any order therein, then you will be guilty of the crime of heresy and be called a heretic. The public pillory is full of them.'

I stayed one more day in the Priory, took some parchment and ink,

1311

and left in the early morning, the first hint of frost crisping the hedges.

Chapter 11
Rose
Tristledermot, 1324 - 1326

There was no peace between my sister and me after that day. When I entered a room, she left. When I spoke she didn't look at me and when I called her name, she didn't answer. My mother refused to take sides. I confided in Brother Francis in the Priory and he said that the destruction of our family had made us both angry, that I should forgive my sister and make the peace of Christ my guiding light. I couldn't do as he asked. It was beyond me.

Women came to the dwelling to ask Eimear for her assistance. She became known the length of the town for her kindness and healing hands. The more the people of the town grew to like her, the more I hated her. She had done what I couldn't do, without as much as two words of Saxon or French to converse with. She had become one of them, present at the births, sharing the sorrows and joys.

Unlike the way of life in the clan, in a town it is possible to avoid a person. I didn't see sight or light of Diarmuid for months. The weekly market still happened, feast days came and went, but there was a black mist in my head. When little Bridín told the stories of the women of the Sídhe, and of the women who were turned into deer and escaped danger, I wished for their fate. Little Bridín was a fair, bright, girl and it was her

Rose

company that I treasured most during those days. She was a nimble seamstress already and was fast and able to learn. She rose early and went into the morning. The people who saw her often gave her goods. She made her own coin doing simple tasks. Carrying water, skinning rabbits or picking stones from green ground. She used the scraps of cloth to make ribbons and finished them well, so that they appeared substantial, and she sold them on market days.

The coin she made, she gave to her grandmother, but sometimes she traded it for curious goods: whale teeth, spoons and combs made of deer horn or other such things. She carried with her always the little figure that Cateline had given her, which she called Maeve, and she made clothes for it.

Since the night I'd spent with Diarmuid, I couldn't play music. My mother said that our dwelling had become like a place of eternal mourning. I was without sleep and without ease. Anger came on my mother. She had grown weary of my company.

'You have little to be grieving. A man is only flesh and bones and no different to any other, when he's in the grave. What darkness is on you and how much longer is it to be on this house?'

She was in sore distress but I couldn't answer her. We heard Eimear's light step. She was still smiling when she entered and then changed her face to a scowl.

'You're as stubborn as each other. I will not live another day like this.'

My mother hit the table with force and marched to the outbuilding.

1324 - 1326

The night was clear and cold.

'Get to your bed, Bridín,' I said.

We made a reluctant truce. It wasn't to last but it brought my mother back inside to the heat.

It was the feast of Samhain, a night when it was traditional for us to burn great fires that marked the end of the light half of the year and grudgingly acknowledged the beginning of the dark half. It was a night when restless souls and Pucaí, and all who lived in the Sídhe mounds, could tramp the land without restriction. That year there would be no fire in our clan and, if those from the underworld went looking for our people, they would have to search far and wide to find them.

In the town, people went to the Abbey to offer prayers for the dead, and I did the same. I was sure my mother and Eimear were of one mind with me but we did not go together. Cateline was full with child but not so far along that she was confined. When she asked me to accompany her to the Governor's dance that night in the castle, I was glad to get out of the house.

The Governor didn't hide away in fear of the wandering ghosts, but instead made the night one of gaiety. There was wine and music and dancing, and in the barrack yard was a roaring fire. The music was his own kind but there was a fiddle player, and a harpist who played our dances. For all his denouncements of the festival of Samhain, the Governor's feast was scattered with it.

Cateline knew of my night with the mason and of my misery since then. She said that a stonemason was not a good match, that I should wed a man with means, that I would lose my independence if I married a man of lesser standing than myself. Her words were small comfort. She was blossoming and I tried to make her night a merry one.

The harpist was a finished musician. I could hear no place where his playing could be improved upon and the fiddler was almost as accomplished. I was lost in the intricate tune when a strange man's voice asked me to dance.

'You can't know this dance, sir. It's an unusual one from the south.'

'You can show me.'

'You'd need a better dancer than me to show you, and it would require more than a single evening to teach it.'

'I learn quickly, and, if you would spend more than one evening with me, it would make me very happy.'

The man was red-haired, green-eyed and of good height. His clothes were well cut and straight stitched. His face wasn't familiar. He was well fed and clean; even his teeth were shining. He was from the next town, he said, and staying a few days.

Cateline was speaking with a woman and she couldn't hear what he was saying. I had no desire to dance. And then, at the doorway, I saw Diarmuid. Most of the women looked his way. Eimear was right about that. The music changed pace and people flocked to the floor.

The man offered his hand and I took it in haste. I tried my best to avoid Diarmuid, but my heart was whispering his name. His eyes found mine but I looked away quickly. I threw myself all the more into the dance. As the night grew late, Cateline tired. Before we left my dance partner inquired my name.

'I will be seeing you again, Rose, I will return to you.'

Cateline rolled her eyes upwards and we walked into the chilly air.

'He's an armourist in the next town, named Walter. His family have a burgage plot and land near Athy.'

'Is he known to you?'

'His sister, Mathilde, is married to the tax collector, Morris.'

All who lived in the town knew Morris. He was a quiet man who would never get wealthy gathering taxes. He was known to be too soft to insist on payment and people took advantage of him. He had been a friend of Jehan's. Those of us who paid what was due in a timely manner were few.

'You've lost interest in the mason? I saw him briefly there tonight.'

I grunted and nodded and we bade each other good night.

If I had known at that time that Walter de White, the armourist, was an acquaintance of Edmond, I would have stayed well away from him. As it was, he found his way to my dwelling not long after Samhain. He had with him an arming coat; a padded coat that was worn beneath armour. The arming coat was buttoned at the front and was double breasted, so that the chest was covered with two layers of the thickly wadded garment. It was for protection and comfort, he told me. Walter wanted me to repair the one he had. He said he had several others that were ripped and needed stitching.

It was heavy work, not the kind I'd choose. There were several

Rose

tailors and tanners in this town and in the next, who were equipped to do what was required with the coats. I knew it was an excuse to see me again. My mother was interested in the identity of the caller, but I didn't enlighten her. I was still too angry with her for not taking my side. Until Eimear came to us, we had been content in our dwelling and in our lives in the town. I agreed to take the coat, telling Walter to return the following week to collect it.

'You'll need thick hooks and threads for that tear,' my mother groused at me.

'I'll get all I need from the tailor. It's my own piece of work and doesn't concern you.'

There was no more said about it. Eimear was busy with the women from the town. There were many infants to deliver. Payment was seldom plentiful. If there was a stillbirth, or a mother died, she would take no coin. And often she paid for prayers at the Abbey for the women she looked after. If the birth was fruitful, and the woman was wealthy, the payment was substantial, but from day to day it was hard to make a steady living from the business of midwifery.

Little Bridín was already making simple gowns. My mother suggested that the girl learn the craft of dressmaking. Bridín showed no interest in babies but, even so, I was surprised when Eimear agreed that ours was the best trade for her daughter to learn. Eimear was often out. I thought it was due to the number of babies being born. She was regularly late, and sometimes didn't come back at all at night. We used to joke, when we were close, that babies always preferred to sneak into

1324 - 1326

the house at night, and that the first sleepless night was usually the night of the birth.

The bakers were found guilty of tampering with the bread. It was short of the weights agreed by the guild, and they had used bad flour with grit. The Governor, who was usually lenient, was outraged. He held up the bakers as an example to all others and, in the early days of that winter, in the cold and bitter wind, he ordered that the six bakers of the town be dipped in the ducking pool. The pool was rarely used for such a punishment. I was told that at one time it had been used to shame immoral women but that did not happen in my time.

Everyone stepped out to watch the spectacle. It had the appearance of fun, and people laughed raucously as the bakers wailed in the icy water.

'It's unkind, Roisín, isn't it?' said little Bridín.

Mathew, the baker, and his wife were good people. Many a morning they had given Bridín a loaf for sweeping the road outside their shop. When they were next in line, their heads were bowed. Mathew was dressed in undergarments and his wife, May, was crying. He spoke softly to her.

'It's just water, May. Go quietly into it and there will be no sport for them. It will be over quick, my love.'

She was tied to a stool at one end of the long ducking board. The middle of the board was set upon a platform and three men used their weight as a lever at the other end, to rise and drop the victim, like a see-saw. May closed her eyes and waited to be dipped.

Rose

'Hold tight, May, sweet pie!' a man jeered.

'Use your loaf next time, May,' a woman shouted, and the crowd laughed.

'My little flower, May, do drop in soon.'

May, who had continued to cry all the while, stopped her tears and then to my astonishment, smiled at the joke. Little Bridín squeezed my hand and the mocking of the crowd changed in an instant.

'You show them, May,' a woman yelled.

The crowd, that had seemed so cruel to us, clapped their hands. The goading stopped and instead there were words of admiration and a surge of warmth. It was as if we had all defied something, and in that moment we were united. The victims, the crowd, even the Governor and his men. I will never understand what it was that happened, but the ducking pond was never used again.

Walter de White seemed to have an endless number of things that needed stitching. He was attentive and pleasant and I came to look forward to his visits. He broke the vicious silence that dwelt between Eimear and me and sometimes I even forgot that it had ever been there.

It was almost Christmas day before I realised that it was Diarmuid who was keeping my sister out late. Little Bridín told me that when she was abroad early one morning, fetching water for the bakers and butchers, she went to see the new heavy horses in the barrack yard. The animals were white with patches of grey or brown, and everyone admired them. That morning, Bridín saw her mother and Diarmuid sleeping in the barn beside the horses. One of the Governor's men shouted at the girl to clear off, and she ran home to tell me what she'd seen.

'Is there something wrong with my mother, Roisín? Why was she there with Diarmuid? Why were they not here? I can sleep at the fire; they can have my bed.'

My mother heard this talk and, when Eimear appeared again, there were harsh words.

'It's no way to bring up a daughter, lying with a man in the barrack yard. We cannot live like that here. The whole town must know of it by now.'

Eimear said that she didn't give a damn what the town knew. She was in love with Diarmuid and they would be married as soon as they had a place to live.

'And what of his people? Where are they?'

'They're in Kilkenny.'

Eimear looked at me. Her face was pale and miserable. I couldn't believe what I was hearing. How could he have lain with her in the place where we'd had such a union? I felt as if all I knew had been burnt to the ground again.

'Well, you'll have to join them there,' I said.

With this my mother lost her temper.

'You'd rather see your sister sleep in a barn than offer her, and the man who would be her husband, shelter under your own roof. That's not the way you were reared. Stay out of my sight, the lot of you. We'll be ruined this way.'

Little Bridín started to cry, believing herself to be the cause of the trouble. I held her close, knowing my mother was right and feeling utterly despondent. I brought the child with me to the Abbey where I confided in Father Michael. He spoke of forgiveness and the love of Jesus. He said that trials like this come to us so we can understand what He meant when He said, *harden not your hearts*. My heart had hardened and it was only acts of love that would soften it again, he said. I was sick of all love.

We stayed in the sanctuary of the shrine. Our Lady of the Sorrows kept us in her downcast gaze. She had witnessed the crucifixion of her only son and still she composed herself afterwards and did what was required of her.

Little Bridín rested her head against my arm. Her little body fell limp as she slept. I lifted her upon my lap, brushed her hair back, and cradled her in my arms. She snored lightly, the sound and the warmth of her deeply comforting. Peace settled on me; I knew what I had to do.

The marriage ceremony of Eimear and Diarmuid was a simple one. Eimear wore the rescued dress she'd used for her first wedding. I'd stitched it myself. My mother, Diarmuid's Uncle Simon, Cateline, Bridín and I went to the Abbey early in the morning, to Father Michael, before the rest of the masons were even stirring in their dormitories. I'd seen Diarmuid once before the wedding, on the day prior to it. The others were gone to make an offering. He'd come to apologise.

1324 - 1326

'For what?'

'I never came back to you, after that night.'

'Don't mind it now. I've forgotten about it. It was nothing.'

My voice shook. Pride is an unsteady refuge.

'Was it nothing?' he asked.

I wanted to know what had occurred but couldn't say it.

'The morning afterwards, something happened…'

'Don't bother with it now, Diarmuid, all that's behind us.'

'Petronella de Midi had a sister, Felicia. After the flogging, people turned on her. They said Petronella had used the buttock hair of a dead boy to make a poison potion and the family of the dead boy wanted even more vengeance. Felicia was alone in Kilkenny and sought help from my family. They concealed her, but then sent her to me and my uncle.'

I could see no purpose in his talk, but it was the most I'd ever heard him say. His eyes rested on mine and my heart began to open to him again.

'She was dressed as a boy and I was tasked with taking her to Dublin port. We went by night, and on foot, on account of the raids. I told my uncle to tell you that I was sorry for my absence, and that I loved you, and that I planned to be back as soon as I could. Uncle Simon couldn't say where I'd gone. To the other masons from Kilkenny, he said that I was called home for family matters. My uncle mistakenly told Eimear, instead of you, what I'd said. When I returned she happened to be at *The Garter Inn*, where she was taking care of one of the innkeeper's nieces. She was overjoyed to see me. I soon realised what had transpired. Then

Rose

I saw you that night in the Governor's, with Walter, and I left things as they were, I never told her about what happened between us.'

'That sounds like a tale that a child would tell, Diarmuid. Don't speak to me about it again. It's in the past now.'

If it weren't so painful, it might have been funny. The feelings I had towards Eimear and Diarmuid changed. It wasn't her fault, Simon had been a poor messenger. But I was haunted by what might have been. It was difficult to adjust to the new arrangements. Patrick built a bed by the fire, and from the wooden beams we hung drapes. In this way the bed of the newly married pair was kept separate from the rest of the room. They were happy with their union and, although I tolerated their joy, I did not share it.

Walter returned to collect his finished arming coat; a *gambeson* he called it. My mother talked about the wedding and inquired about his family and business.

'Much can happen in a week,' she said.

Walter agreed and winked at me. I didn't love him, but he was a handsome young man and I welcomed his attention. It was something to lean on while my heart was so unreliable.

Cateline was blessed with an infant girl, and Eimear guided both mother and child safely into a dark evening. She was a radiant little one, whom Cateline named Eva.

Winter that year was wet and mild. The rivers and streams rose above

1324 - 1326

their banks and silver floods lay heavily on the land around the town. Many of us had newly tiled roofs by this time, and we were glad of them that year. Walter was a generous suitor. He travelled between Tristledermot and Athy twice a month and brought goods from the Athy market, as well as small curiosities for little Bridín. When the rain persisted during the short hours of light, the stone masons had little work to do. My mother instructed Diarmuid to fix the outbuildings and hen house, and perform any work she could think of to occupy him, for he got under her feet when he was idle. I liked the wet days and his company. It was impossible not to enjoy it. He was good-natured, kind and quick-witted. Diarmuid always had a hopeful view of things and passed on this view to anyone in his presence, yet I remained torn between the love, regret and jealousy that I felt but could not speak of.

Walter bought a wooden flute for Bridín. It was carved and hollowed from a hazel branch. The sound was delicate, light notes followed the rhythm of the breath. Little by little I taught her my father's tunes.

The Sunday before Saint Brighid's day was a dark one. We were making crosses from rushes, which we would bring to be blessed. Diarmuid's uncle came to visit, as had become his custom. My mother cut bread for him and thickly buttered it.

'The work of the masons is almost complete here, there's just enough work for two men now. There's talk of a wealthy family in Kilkenny, who want a chapel built. If we leave tomorrow, we should be well employed in our own town for a number of years.'

Rose

'Tomorrow?'

'Our reputation has gone before us. We've been sent for, but we have to be quick.'

Diarmuid and Eimear stared at each other. My mother was quiet. Little Bridín asked her mother if this meant that she was to leave the town. Diarmuid answered her;

'We will leave this place, but we'll go to another town, bigger than this one.'

The child argued with her mother, until she could see that there was no budging her. She withdrew to her bed and sobbed. My mother began to ask practical questions. What would Eimear need to take with her? Would there be a place for them to live? How would they travel so far? She spoke then about the child.

'Be careful about dragging her that distance with you. If she remains with us she'll learn a good trade.'

'I can't leave without her, Mother.'

But we knew from that moment that the child would stay with us.

'Leave her for a couple of years. She can join you then.'

Diarmuid was silent, knowing not to interfere in the arrangements but, like us all, he was upset. I took great comfort in knowing that the child would remain, but was deeply wounded by the revelation of Diarmuid and Eimear's departure. I knew it was unlikely that I'd see them again in this life.

Many of the masons left on the same day. It's safer to travel long distances in great numbers. Several of the carts of the town were employed to carry them and, on account of the trouble abroad, many hired men of arms were to accompany the procession. It was a stray bright day between bouts of bad weather that year. Cateline and Eva came out to see off the travellers; Eva was thriving and had found her voice.

I asked Father Michael to bless the crosses in advance of Saint Brighid's day and I gave them to Diarmuid, Eimear and Simon in the new morning. Our dwelling was quiet again then, after the departure, as the three of us turned our attention to the work before us. The following days were interrupted by women looking for Eimear, but it wasn't long before word went through the town and the women went elsewhere.

Walter de White came to the market that week. The cattle plague was still picking off the last of the herds in the south. Every province was cursed with it. It meant that the market still had none of the goods that were reliant on provision by cattle, but other things were on offer. Shoes of horse and goat leather, and other animal skins not usually used by the tanner, were studied by Bridín, who wandered away to gaze at all the wares.

Walter found me alone at our stall in the square. He took a large cloak from my table that was made in our own style and wrapped it about himself. He looked Irish in it. His wild red hair reminded me of Brion. Sometimes the dead stand next to me. It used to frighten me but since the burning of our clan, I treasure the moments when I feel them

Rose

so near. I could sense Brion's hand upon my shoulder and hear his teasing.

'You'll never thatch a roof with himself. He's only a wisp of hay standing in for a thick sheaf.'

I smiled and Walter took it that I was pleased with what I saw.

'I'll take this cloak and, if it satisfies you, I'll take the seller with it!'

'The cloak makes a cosy nest for the wearer beneath it. The maker of the cloak is not for sale.'

Walter laughed at this and we bargained over the mantel. He gave me a fair price for the piece. He wore it that very day and I consented to accompany him to meet his family in the next town. We agreed the date of travel would be the following Sunday.

The next town wasn't as well fortified as our own. Some months previously, and not for the first time, Athy had suffered at the hands of the O'Moores. Buildings were still without roofs, part of the wall was destroyed and two of the gates were waiting for repair. Walter's large family was living within one dwelling. Apart from his sister, Mathilde, they all lived together. His two brothers and their wives, six children and his father. His mother had died at Mathilde's birth.

I was well received by the de Whites and we dined on goose but, when it was time to leave, I was glad to go. They spoke of the wild Irish, in my presence, as if we were mere animals to be herded, managed and disposed of. They said that we married as and when we liked and divorced just as quickly and that we had no regard for either the rules of the church or the law.

There wasn't a space in the dwelling where another person's leg or foot wasn't brushing against my own. They were seldom all home at the one time however, Walter told me. The other men oversaw the farming, and he was most often in the armoury next to the dwelling. He showed me the weapons and armour. His workshop was within a thick walled building, behind two solid, locked doors. Walter showed me crossbows and swords, metal suits of armour and a row of gambesons. There were boots and all manner of ropes and chains. His face was happy as he described the functions of the implements, but I didn't find any entertainment in it. It was a cold, savage collection of things.

Growing old in the town was easier than it had been in the clan but, just as an apple bud flowers, ripens and falls, there's no escaping the way the weight of the years bends us and lays us with the worms in our graves. My mother was burdened with the tiredness of her age. Her back was now stooped and her eyes were weak. It was a blessing for her to have little Bridín to thread needles and fetch warm stones wrapped in cloths to place next to her cold feet. It saddened me to see her suffer. Eimear's leaving had taken some of her strength. What little was left, she used as best she could to contribute to the keeping of the house.

Ava next door ensured that we had a supply of good light bread. I mixed it with honey, milk and eggs and cooked it to encourage my mother to eat. Her appetite was fading too. She taught little Bridín all she knew of dress making and the final gown that my mother created

Rose

was to be the last dress she wore. Bridín completed it quickly. It was made from fair linen and I was instructed to sew the familiar patterns of our family onto the wide trim at the neck and hem.

I stitched a Saint Brighid's cross and the three red stones of Saint Ita into the pattern. When Bridín described the embroidery to my mother, the new symbols pleased her. She started to speak more of her own parents and grandparents, of old Áine and of all who were killed of our family. It was as if she were calling on them to accompany her on her final journey, through the lonely passage from this world to the next.

Her decline was swift. She woke one morning and was unable to rise from the bed. She stopped eating and only sucked lukewarm water from a piece of cloth. She used the last of her voice to utter prayers and a loving farewell to us. Father Michael came to administer the sacrament of extreme unction, the final anointing, and after this, she slipped into silence, breathing slowly until she took her final precious breath.

Until my mother died, I believed I had known my fair share of heartbreak, but I was wrong. The pain I felt when she passed away was like none other, not the loss of Tomás or Jehan or Diarmuid – not even the loss of my clan – compared with the piercing wound of my mother's death. I could hear her voice, at every turn, in my mind. In the mornings, I could hear her say a prayer before I even opened my eyes. She followed her prayer with words of encouragement to get me out of the cot.

'You're lucky you were born an O'Byrne. There's no use in

mourning as if spring is never to come again. A handful of skill is better than a bag full of gold, now get to work.'

I resisted her coaxing, asking her to let me grieve a while; I was too wretched to pretend to be happy. But she didn't listen and continued on. As little Bridín needed me to comfort her too I moved with her, as best I could, through that time.

Walter de White had kept his distance while my mother was ill, and I was grateful for that. He attended the funeral and made an offering to the Abbey to continue their prayers for her soul. Geoffrey was still keeping order on our green ground and Walter gave him seedlings to plant and he mended our shovel and rake. Walter also brought flower seeds for Bridín and helped her to sow them. He seemed a good man, although Geoffrey told me he'd thumped him thrice. I didn't pay much heed to that; there were times recently when Geoffrey had been lazy.

Walter called late one night. The weather had turned and he wasn't going to travel back to Athy. I said he could stay on the bed by the fire and he was content with this offer. We talked into the night while the child was sleeping.

'It could be like this every night, Rose, if we were wedded.'

It was a sensible suggestion. So much recently had made no sense and Walter could make a good husband. My heart wasn't singing for him but all was flat and dull for me at that time. My mother used to say to me that it was on me to marry soon again, if I wanted children, and I

Rose

did want children.

'The lease on this dwelling is my own; it was negotiated with the Governor after my husband died.'

'There would be no change in that regard, Rose, and I would have to go to the armoury still in the next town. There's plenty of work for me in Athy.'

He grew excited at the thought of our marriage and it did me good to hear his enthusiasm for the future. I told him I hoped for children.

'A clutch of boys and girls to gather about us; what more could we ever want?' he said and kissed me. His lips were coarse from wind and rain but he was kind and made me feel safe.

We were wed three weeks after that. On three consecutive Sundays our intention to wed was announced. Bridín made green ribbons for us both, which she'd embroidered with ivy leaves and holly. I looked closely at mine and saw that she'd stitched pairs of tiny hands between the berries. It was just like something I might make. When I told her this, she beamed and held me. She was truly a blessing from God.

The first night of our marriage Walter and I spent in the bed by the fire. Walter was loving, awakening in me again the pleasure of making love. He tenderly caressed my arms, kissed my neck and even my knees. I laughed at the ticklish touch of his fingertips along the backs of my legs. He kissed my breasts and stayed with his tongue moving feverishly between my legs, until I thought I would burst with pleasure. He put himself inside me and thrust himself rhythmically until his seed erupted within me. He gazed into my eyes and then whispered so faintly and coldly that I thought I had misheard him.

'It will never be like this again.'

He turned away from me and fell asleep, snoring loudly. The firelight was still flickering in the rafters. Stored under the eave was my old wedding dress. I hadn't used it to marry Walter. I had never slept in this bed either and suddenly my own dwelling felt like a strange place. A mouse ran along the shortest beam in the room; I decided to ask Geoffrey to find a cat for us. My mother hated cats so we never had them about the place. I had always detested mice.

When the nuns in Grane had heard of my sister's skills at midwifery, they used to send for her whenever a midwife was needed in the nunnery. The nun, who called to fetch her on the Ash Wednesday after she'd gone, was disappointed to hear she'd left.

'She has hands of life; she delivered all our babies in the past year. We'll be lost without her.'

'I miss her too,' I said. I hadn't believed it until that morning. The nun, Sister Beatrice, recognised Bridín.

'You haven't taken the path of your mother?'

'No, I'm a dressmaker.' Bridín answered.

Bridín gave the young nun a ribbon that she'd just completed. Beatrice was delighted with it.

'Could you make one with my name sewn onto it?'

'I can't read.'

'Then you must come to Grane and learn.'

It was a fine opportunity for the child.

'She can go on the cart that leaves each evening and return the following morning. I need her to work during the day.'

'So be it, she can come to me tomorrow evening.'

Bridín began to object, but I silenced her.

'Thank you kindly, Sister Beatrice. She's a good girl and will make a worthy student.'

Fear is the servant of an angry man. With Bridín gone at night the house was quieter than it had ever been. I used to stare for hours into the flames after the day was over. When Walter came, it was always late. I tried to talk to him about what he'd said that night but he denied saying anything at all.

I was glad Bridín was out of the house on those nights. The first time after the wedding night that he'd made love to me, he was rough in his manner. I tried to touch his skin but he brushed my hand away and snapped at me.

'Don't move your hand like that.'

He bit my neck with force and hurt me. When I asked him to stop he did it again. The shock of it froze me like a river in deep winter. And then with no tenderness or gentle caresses, he grasped my breasts and squeezed them sorely. When he put himself inside me I was dry and it caused me sharp pain.

'Walter, stop yourself; you're hurting me!'

'Shut up, woman, and don't speak or touch me. Lie still and let me finish, whore.'

It was unlike anything that had happened ever before. I thought of Cateline. I'd heard women speak of cold men and now I understood what they meant. Walter satisfied himself, turned over and slept. I went to my old sleeping room and climbed into the bed, where my mother used to lie. I missed her words of wisdom more than ever. I had made such a terrible mistake in marrying again.

This happened many times over the following months. Sometimes he made himself pleasant the day after these unions. On those days he spoke as if all were well, and I wondered if I was imagining his cruelty. He brought gifts, food and offered me coin that I didn't take. Other times he would tell me that his family had thought it beneath him to marry an Irish woman, but that he'd told them he'd pitied me. When he spoke it was often in a false voice, as if he were a fool at the market place. I felt undone of the charms that had once made me a woman of mystery, and I grew nervous every evening as night approached, never knowing when he'd arrive.

It was the feast of Saint John and the monks in the Priory were holding a day of prayer. I went with Cateline and the baby. We had never spoken about the black eye she'd had or about Walter's cruelty.

We didn't manage to talk about it that night either. When I returned home, Walter was in my dwelling and he wasn't alone. Edmond and a woman were sitting at my table.

'Here is my wife now. Where have you been, my pet?'

Rose

Edmond laughed at this, and said that I'd been out at *The Garter Inn*, where I was often seen drinking with the men, like the rest of the wild Irish. They all cackled at this. I wanted to turn and run, but couldn't leave them in the dwelling for fear of what they might do. I offered them bread and hot milk but they asked for ale. I went to the outbuilding to get the ale, every part of me trembling with rage and fear. Suddenly Walter's cruelty made sense. He was in league with Edmond. I knew that things would be worse by morning, when the rest of the ale would be drunk.

Walter was loud. 'Stay and drink with us, Rose, pet. Fill up their cups. Don't spare the ale; we're practically related to Edmond. Make this a home for yourselves, friends.'

Edmond found this uproarious.

'And I'm sorry about your mother, Rose, although a man can rest easier without her here.' Edmond's words were slurred but cutting.

'It'd be better for me if you'd leave, Edmond, and take your friend with you, although I have no fight to pick with her.'

Walter was poking the fire and he stopped and turned. His eyes were those of another man. It was as if my dwelling were under attack by raiders. He shouted at me to shut up and do as I was bid, that he was the man of the house and I had better bend to his will. He said that the house was his, now that I had remarried, and that I was to get used to the new arrangement. I realised then that he wasn't going to be bested by me with Edmond there looking on.

If I spoke again, he'd surely strike me. I sat and Edmond's friend chattered and then Edmond spoke.

'You know that Walter is the godfather of Jehan's daughter. It was to be Morris who stood for her, but he was ill and sent Walter in his stead.'

'No, I didn't know that. How is the girl?'

'With her mother, in Dublin. Adeline is to be married soon.'

Talk of Adeline seemed to calm Edmond, but Walter was sulking since his outburst. I knew when he got his moment, he would make his fury felt. The tension in the house was sickening.

Walter stood behind me; I felt his penis pressing into my back. I sat very still, unsure of what to do. He put his hand on my head and then clenched his fingers until he was pulling my hair tight.

'Come now, pet, apologise to our guests.'

The woman stood to leave; Edmond finished his ale and winked at me.

'We'll let you get on with the business of marriage.'

I hoped I would fall faint before they left.

'I'll recount the business of the night when I see you next,' Walter said.

The two men laughed at this, the sound was as of pigs grunting. Edmond and the woman left and the terror of my heart filled the house.

I had never been struck by a man before. The force of his strength was like that of a horse. By the time he was on me, I was rigid with disgust and cold fear. It was as if I had left my body and become the mouse who was still wandering about in the rafters.

Rose

He was gone early the next morning. All day I told myself that it hadn't really happened, and that was an easier way to get on with the work at hand. There was much to do. I had never felt so broken nor so alone.

In the end it was the nuns who came to my aid. Sister Beatrice, as if sent by God, arrived to my dwelling with Bridín. She had kept the girl late. Bridín was gifted at letters and at numbers and Sister Beatrice liked her company at the market stall, where Bridín seemed to be able to account for every coin spent and every item traded.

Sister Beatrice was explaining this to me when she stopped her words and noticed the bruises on my face. The first thing she did was implore Saint Brighid to intercede on my behalf with Our Lord. The second thing she did was send Bridín to the baker for fresh bread. As soon as Bridín was out the door, Sister Beatrice asked me what had happened and I was unable to say anything but the truth. I told her all, even of Walter's other cruelties in our bed. Knowing my desire for a baby, he had stopped spilling his seed within me and emptied it instead upon me.

'There's no hope of children between us.'

'God was wise to keep them from you. We won't have this any longer.'

Afterwards Cateline told me that the nuns at Grane were known for solving the problems of bad marriages in the town. I didn't ask her about her own situation; perhaps mine was worse than most. In any case it was my good fortune that Eimear and Bridín were so well thought of in the nunnery, and it was to my advantage that I had kept a strong bond with the Abbey.

Sister Beatrice complained to the Abbot that the marriage between Walter de White and Rose Darcy was not binding. She said that we were blood relations on account of Walter being the godfather of Jehan's daughter. She said that spiritual and blood affinity was against the rule of consanguinity and that we'd had no permission to marry. She ordered a man of law to draw up a document that would dissolve the marriage and then complained to the Governor about Walter de White and said that the Abbess of Grane requested that Walter de White be denied entry to the town. And neither he nor Edmond were ever to be served in *The Garter Inn* again. I hadn't known that the inn was owned by the nuns of Grane. I realised, after speaking with Cateline, that the nuns were in possession of the title deeds of most of the town buildings.

There was a garrison at the nunnery, so Sister Beatrice sent the document to Walter with the men of arms from Grane. He was to stay away from Tristledermot. I didn't see Walter after that terrible night and, before the summer had crept into autumn that year, I was again the widow Darcy. I offered thanks to the Abbey and to the nuns of Grane who had saved me from ruin. All through that winter and into the spring again, I could hear my mother's voice say, 'I told you that you were lucky to have been born an O'Byrne.'

Chapter 12
Brother John
Bristowe and Europe, 1312 - 1348

To survive the winter I offered my services to the small leper hospital that was attached to the convent of Saint Mary Magdalene in the town. In return for assisting with the sick, I was given my food and board. Agnes had advised me that the handful of nuns, whose duty it was to provide for the dying, were always in need of help. I shared my duties with another monk who had left his order and a lay man. We held the hands of many men and women who perished from different forms of the disease, and then we carried them to their graves and prayed alongside the nuns for the deliverance of their souls to Our Lord. The leper hospital was financed by the town dues and funds from the larger convents in the land. There was no waste and no outward show of affluence. It soothed my spirit and helped to keep alive my vow of poverty. I left the leper hospital when the weather improved.

Bristowe in the summer is coloured with emeralds and sapphires. The distant gorge and the land in our sight were every shade of green, and the river and sky were blue reflections of each other. There were long days of light in which to visit the sick. Although Agnes had invited me to stay with her family, I declined the offer. Her father had trouble enough and in any case he didn't seem pleased that his daughter had fixed her attention on a failed, foreign scribe. Agnes showed me to the place where those without homes sometimes resided in the town. A cave-like structure where the dock men and seasonal workers slept.

I spent my days with the poor beyond the walls, speaking God's words, baptising babies and burying souls who, for the most part, were departing early from this world. I had no sanction from any church, but there were no others performing the rituals, save the midwives, if they were present. I heard confessions, although I had no licence to do so, but the people who asked me to absolve them of their sins said that they were outside of the parish and beyond the help of the church. Their sins weren't different from those found within a town. Theft, adultery, lying, fornication, covetousness, greed, murder, infanticide – but gluttony was never mentioned. When I said that I didn't have the authority to administer the sacraments, I was told that the church didn't punish those who helped the poor. As long as a man wasn't diverting money from the pockets of the clergy, he would be left alone. They were right in that regard but I was sure that it would only be a matter of time before a complaint would be made against me. Without an order I was no different from a lay man.

I refused food if offered, but I did accede to Agnes's insistent request to join her family for the evening meal. A good meal, once daily, was more than most of the poor could hope for and I was very grateful for her generosity.

The wool merchant gave me sporadic employment, writing letters on his behalf to mariners and others associated with his trade, and I gave the money to the poor beyond the gate. I was as happy as I could ever hope to be until the crop failed that year.

I knew famine. It was a constant threat and it was true that I had seen the poor die of hunger, but nothing could have prepared me for the misery of that time. In Tristledermot the numbers of people were easier to feed. In a city the demands of the population were beyond what could be met. The city council issued decrees that anyone stealing food would be hanged. The gates were locked and the knights, who had looked so noble on their dazzling horses, were ordered to control the starving crowds by use of force.

The Magdalene nuns and the people of the district made huge pots of broth for the paupers of the parish, but they didn't extend their hospitality beyond the walls.

'There simply isn't enough to go around,' Agnes said.

It was a pitiful sight and one that I will never forget. The numbers overwhelmed me and it became impossible to continue to offer comfort to the dying. I was given a choice by the guards at the gate, who by this time knew me well – either leave the town and remain outside the walls, or stay within until the council decreed otherwise. If it was a further test of my faith and commitment, I failed miserably, to my shame.

The famine did pass and, after the dead had been buried in great pits, the town opened again, but the fear of hunger stayed in the air. I passed years in the town living between the hospital, the cave and Agnes's table. The year of famine was followed by a run of good harvests and then the cattle plague struck and the scale of it caused more suffering again among the poor.

Agnes grew from a girl into womanhood. After her father died, it fell to her to keep the house. When her brother came of age, the house would be passed to him. Her brother had learned much of their father's trade, and was now apprenticed to a smith, where he would complete his learning. I often wondered when she would marry and then I had no need to wonder anymore.

Before Agnes told me of her suitor, we walked the road to the Temple Church, where people sat in the yard on warm evenings. I never became familiar with the parish divisions in the city. There seemed to be so many and each had its own church. I knew the parish priest of the Temple Church, Father Anselm. He was a good man and used to ensure that I had clothing, blessed water and oil for my work beyond the walls. He used to jest that no man could count the orders of clerics, and that disagreements among the many forms of religious life were more frequent and vicious than those among lay-people. Father Anselm, who always wore a horsehair vest, had no time for the clergy of Saint James' Priory.

Agnes's skin was clear and beautiful and I had to resist again the urge to touch her hair.

'You have been a monk without a monastery for a long time now, Fabien. When will you find a home again?'

'When there's no need for me here.'

'You bring succour to the sick and dying. The people all speak well of you but you can't live like this all your life. You must get tired of living without coin and of the smells and sickness and complaints of the poor.'

Agnes had never understood the vow of Saint Augustine. In a town like this one, it was seldom practised. All those years ago, when I'd met the old monk who'd travelled to the Holy Land, he'd told me that he'd heard it said in the east, that a person who can't live in this world without coin is not free. His words impressed me deeply.

'With or without coin, I'm the same man.'

'You are a stubborn monk. You'd make a good husband if you ever thought of marrying.'

A lonely ache, like an old friend, touched my heart and reminded me of how much I loved Agnes. I was a stubborn man; the surety of my faith crumbled into doubt yet again.

'I would be a poor husband, giving away all I'd earned before I ever reached home.'

Agnes put her hand on mine, as she liked to do. It was as light a touch as a bird's and as strong as a pillar. When twilight hung its deepening violet shawl over the city, Agnes and I strolled hand in hand back to her dwelling. In her empty house we kissed. Her lips were soft petals on mine. I traced the shape of her body with my hands and she moved herself against me. My reason was warning me against lust but my senses were starving for her love.

'You really do stink,' she laughed and released me. She sat the large round pail on the floor, took warm water that had been sitting in a pot near the glowing embers and told me to undress and stand in it. I hadn't stood naked before a woman since boyhood. The soap and warm water were exquisite.

'Your clothing is filthy and threadbare.'

She laid out her father's clothes. I had never worn a lay man's garments. She said that she would wash my clothes. The habit I wore was a Hospitallers one, grey undyed wool that had been given to me, along with a cowl and my well-worn shoes, by Father Anselm. I no longer had the cross of my order. It was as if, bit by bit, I was shedding my vows.

I was aroused, standing in the pail, with Agnes's hands upon my skin, but I'd misread again the nature of our encounter.

'Would you like to lie with a woman, Fabien?'

'I would like to lie with you, Agnes,'

She kissed me and I tried again to touch her. She gave me cloth to dry myself. And then she told me of the man she was thinking of wedding. A smith, like her father, whom she'd known since childhood. I was embarrassed by my unhidden desire.

'I don't understand women, Agnes.'

'I thought that perhaps, before I married, I might offer you that which has always been denied to you.'

'Denied by you?'

'By women, Fabien.'

'But it is my vows that keep me from women, Agnes, not people. I'm the only one, with God's grace, who can keep the vows I took and I'm the only one who can break them.'

I knew she thought I was peculiar. It was so unusual for any man or woman to be celibate, despite the rules of orders. I was again disappointed. The passion had left me when I heard that Agnes was to be married. If my life had been different, Agnes would have been the only woman I would have chosen to be with. I wanted to tell her this but I was unable to find the power to utter the words. I kept my counsel instead with Father Anselm, who called me a fool, a saint, and a blathering goat, and slapped me on the head when I told him what had happened.

Knights and mercenaries were stationed in abundance in the town. Wealthy people had their own men of arms and the Earl employed knights, many of whom were the landless sons of the powerful. Fights were common in the ale houses, especially in times of peace. The watchmen and guards of the gates knew everyone, even occasional visitors and, when there was trouble in the town, it was the gate guards who were called on first to intervene.

I often sat at the Green watching the drinking men leave at night. If I saw a fray, it helped me to remember why the religious life suited me, although I didn't choose it as such. Circumstances brought me to it and habit kept it at the centre of my life. All the same, without an order to be guided by, the discipline that I'd once enjoyed had become harder to execute. I no longer rose at the strike of four bells for prayer. I didn't

Brother John

keep silence with any regularity, although there were times when without a companion I didn't talk. I missed the comradeship of the monastery and the laughter of my brothers. In the silence of a monastery, God's voice is heard. Brother Francis used to say that God didn't speak in words but in the intuition we felt in our souls throughout the day. He said that silence opened the gates of heaven within us and, once opened, God could freely reach us through them. It had been so long since I had kept the hours of my order that the gates of heaven within me felt closed.

Agnes married the smith and was already with child. Her attention was on her husband now and I seldom saw her. Once the child arrived she would be absorbed in the life she'd chosen. The passage of time is the maker of change. My closeness to Agnes was coming to an end and I was deserted. Brother Francis used to say that the Lord is our only true companion, but I don't think he tried to live among the people. Friends are the refuge of the lonely.

I had been years in the town when I met the Pilgrimage Knights, as I sat on the Green. They were bound for the Holy Land, they said, and were to accompany a group of pilgrims, whom they were to meet in France. They were young and enthusiastic and their talk of travel infected me. My long abandoned dream rose from their eyes and I asked if it were possible to go with them and they agreed. I had no coin, I told them, but they said that there would be coin enough in France.

1312 - 1348

I became familiar with the anatomy of men through the butchery of the Pilgrimage Knights. They had no interest in finding the Holy Land or of following Jesus. Instead they robbed and maimed in God's name. I thought their offer was too good to be true and this turned out to be the case. The beginning of the pilgrimage was like a festival. It was an annual event that left the north of France and visited far-off shrines on the route to their final destination. Each town we entered welcomed us with food and rough lodgings; the wealthier pilgrims boarding at the inns. By the time we left, the people who lived there were robbed, threatened and hurt. As soon as the pilgrims were accommodated for the night, the villains scouted the area for victims. I heard talk among the townspeople of thievery, and had observed the five knights leaving the town and returning in the early hours the next morning in great spirits. They gambled in the inns, and fought when they lost, taking the coin that they believed to be theirs.

Further along the route, we overtook a company of people. There were two men of arms with the group and those on the cart were well dressed. Sometime later our pilgrims stopped to rest. I followed the knights who retraced their steps until they met again the well-dressed company. From a distance, I saw the villains murder the men of arms and take the coin and gems of the travellers. I hid until the knights went by me and continued to the cart where I saw a man, a woman and a boy bloodied, dead or dying. I went to the woman, who was breathing her last, and absolved her from all past error. Her eyes were on me as I spoke and she was unable to lift her head. In my own tongue, for the victims and myself were of the same mother tongue, I said, 'The boy is going with you, mother. God has prepared a room for you all with Him. May you go in peace where you will be welcomed by the angels in heaven, who will open their arms to you and relieve you of all your suffering.'

The spirit of life left the woman. She was lying in a bath of blood, her own, her son's and her husband's. The others were already dead, but I repeated the final prayers and blessed them. I saw the severed neck of one of the soldiers, the bones and vessels of blood exposed. His hand was diminished by two fingers and the other soldier's foot was no longer where you would expect to see it; instead it was placed on his chest.

My stomach, that Agnes used to say had the strength of an ox, rebelled against the cruelty on display, and I doubled over, retching for a long time. The pain in my breast was severe. How can men commit such attacks on fellow humans? The motives of men change, but the effects of their oppression and cruelty are timeless. My own brother's life was extinguished in the name of war; the lives of these people in the name of faith. For many years my brothers in the crusades left trails of corpses in the name of God.

I walked without caring which direction I travelled in. There is no motive, good or bad, that can justify such evil. Where was my Lord when that family was dying?

When I left that family on the road side, I left behind me all hope of getting to the Holy Land.

1312 - 1348

I shed my habit and monks attire, using instead the traditional clothes of the area that were given to me by kindly women. For years I wandered as a labourer among the land workers, following the growing seasons and harvests. My faith had deserted me, just as my youth had, and I was often desolate. I could no longer hear Saint John or Our Lord guiding my actions. The Lord had indeed been my true companion, and the loneliness and emptiness was now beyond compare. I lay with many women and I agreed with Father Anselm. I had been a blathering goat and a fool.

I saw the years change throughout empires, the long summers of Iberia and the snowy mountains of the north. What coin I made I shared between those who were in need and the procurement of parchment. I was writing on pages that I hoped one day would be bound. I was broken enough by then to know that I had no authority over any man, and no right to offer misguided advice to anyone. I was a quiet listener and it was that skill, along with my labour, that was any value to my fellow workers. I continued to hear confessions, in my own way, but no longer had the power or inclination to absolve a person and I no longer suggested penance. The stories I heard on my journey provided me with ample proof of the suffering endured by people.

Words from my stagnant heart planted themselves on my parchment. I had no need to write prayers. Much of what was written was of anguish and of love, of Agnes. The drawings I made were of scenes I saw about me. For a man in the north I drew his children playing. He

Brother John

compensated me well for my efforts and recommended me to another man, who was equally generous. I copied from nature as I'd copied from the masters' pages in my youth.

I was restless everywhere and more and more my winged dreams flew to Tristledermot, to St John's, to the roots of my lost faith, and the place I called home. Among people I laboured with, I was ashamed to say I was a monk. I saw the comfort that faith afforded them and couldn't speak of my vanished beliefs. Sometimes a person would say,

'You must be a cleric! You have the sure appearance of one.'

I never understood how they could tell, but when it was stated, I denied it as if I were Peter in the Garden.

I found the company of Jews and Saracens tranquil. Knowing I wasn't of their kind, they didn't care what I believed and had no need for the sacraments of the church, so I felt no guilt for not being able to provide them. An old man, Salam, who had been shipped north of his own land in slavery, but who'd escaped, took me as a confidante and friend. He said I didn't eat much, worked hard and was reluctant to preach at him. It was with him that I travelled to lands I'd never heard of, and with him I witnessed many great kindnesses done for no reward. He suited my disposition, although we were often hungry and cold.

When, on a wintery night of snow in the north, he took ill and died, I decided to return to Bristowe. There had been much talk of pestilence. There were many ships docked in the port town of Caletum, in France, where I first witnessed the pestilence. Not seven days after, a woman

1312 - 1348

fell dead with it at the door of the Hospitallers. The sound of people wailing filled the town. The ships were setting sail in a great hurry and it was my good fortune that I was permitted on board to sail for England.

I arrived in Bristowe ahead of the pestilence. I lied in order to persuade the guards to let me through the gate. The town was as busy as ever and more affluent. I made my way straight to Agnes's dwelling, to find her younger brother, now a handsome man, there. He directed me to a dwelling near the Green, where Agnes and her family were living. She was overjoyed to see me. She'd had two broods of children; the first now reared and, with her second husband, she'd had three more. Her youngest daughter was present and so like Bracy in appearance that I almost cried to see her.

'She's too pretty for this world, like my sister,' said Agnes.

'Delicate as the flowers are, they can survive even on snowy mountains.'

'My days of childbirth are over now; she was a precious gift given late to me.'

Agnes noticed my lay clothes and asked why I wasn't wearing a monk's habit.

'Without God, Agnes, there is no monk.'

She laughed at this, and said that the town was full of Godless clergy. One more surely wouldn't make a difference.

Agnes opened a wooden trunk that her daughter, Bela, had been sitting on, and removed a pile of cloth.

Brother John

'When I first met you, Fabien, your robe was blue, I remember the day you sat on the quay, with your red cross over the blue habit. I thought you looked like a knight. Just before you left Bristowe, I promised to wash this for you.'

She handed me my old robe that had been newly dyed rich blue.

'I hope you don't mind, I revived it. The grey was so dirty. And I asked the dressmaker to copy the cross. It's not exactly the same, I'm sure, but it's how I remembered it.'

I couldn't believe that she'd kept it all these years and taken such care with it.

'How did you know I'd be back?'

The sight of my habit moved me intensely, as if holiness were woven into the threads.

'I didn't know; I hoped.'

'It's as if you have returned me to myself, Agnes. Thank you.'

We talked of all the years between us, how young we'd been. She laughed when I admitted my foolishness the last evening I'd spent with her.

'People talked about you fondly for years in this town. They still do and after you left they continued to send for you.'

She smiled, pride in her eyes as she told me this, and although I was honoured to hear of it, I felt unworthy of the praise. The familiar bells were a balm to me and the town guards announcing the curfew gave us the feeling of safety.

'Have you heard about the plague that is coming? Have you seen it?'

Her voice was filled with fear, I heard it in the upward tone, just as a hymn rises as it lifts towards God for succour. She was braiding the little one's hair and Bela was singing to herself.

'No, I haven't seen it; it may not even get this far.'

Agnes arranged lodgings for me at an inn on the Green. From my room I could see her bright blue door. Before the week was out, the pestilence, death's closest companion, had entered the city and together they reaped the best of people, as they had done in every other place.

The guards announced that there was to be no movement of people and all the gates were locked. The inns opened all the same, and I heard both day and night, the merrymaking of the people in the tavern below. The greater the threat of death, the louder and more base the people grew.

To my horror, on a chilly morning, the blue door had drawn upon it a painted red cross, the sign of plague within the house. A cutting pain went through me as I left the inn and the crowd of revellers behind.

'Bring out your dead! Bring out your dead!.'

The cart, which was hauled by an old dark mare and steered by two gravediggers, stopped outside Agnes's dwelling.

'O God, my Lord, Saint John, help them! Take this sickness from the family of Agnes,' I prayed.

The guards who were accompanying the gravediggers warned me to stay away. They too were praying, begging God for His mercy. The door opened and Agnes's three children dragged out the body of their

Brother John

father, which was put upon a board, and then placed onto the cart. And then they returned to the dwelling and dragged another corpse over the threshold and onto the road. Agnes, her hair greying and her face black with blotches, stared unseeing at the sky. I was warned again to keep away and the guards spoke harshly to the children to remain within the dwelling. They asked them if they had sufficient provisions and the children answered that they had, and then retreated. Agnes and her husband were two among a dozen in the cart.

I clambered onto a wheel and made the sign of the cross on the foreheads of Agnes and her husband. Although I didn't believe it mattered, I absolved them of all their previous sins and asked God to make room for them in His house.

Shattered and sick from the cruelty of the world, I hid in the inn for the rest of the day. The next morning the scene was repeated, but this time it was the bodies of the beautiful children who were placed on the cart and carried to their resting place. I prayed that they would be reunited with their parents and I imagined I could hear Agnes speaking to me, just as I had all through my travels and lonely nights. I wanted, more than ever, to go home.

It was my robe, in the end, that granted me a place on the ship. Mariners were loath to take on any passengers, for fear of the pestilence, but were reassured by the cloth of a holy man. I left on the high tide, praying for the souls of Agnes and her family, despite my lack of faith. The sea and prayers soothed my broken heart.

Chapter 13
Rose
Tristledermot, 1326 – 1348

Whatever spirit that had allowed my mother to start anew was also in me. The town grew warm that summer, the harvest was good and there was plenty of produce from our own green ground. Edmond had been warned away from my dwelling and he heeded the Governor's warning. Yet, when I heard a loud noise, or saw or imagined a sudden movement, a wave of panic would sweep through me, leaving me unable to breathe or move for a time. I talked to Cateline of it and she told me that I'd get used to it.

Little Bridín became as fluent with letters and numbers as any man, and she was able to keep account of our trade on parchment. She became confident with the songs and tunes of my father and it was a great comfort to hear her play them. It was she that forced me to pick up my flute again, and she traded her wooden flute for one that was similar to my own. We played together in the long evenings.

She reminded me so much of my sister that Eimear was never far from my mind. I remembered our time as children, with our mother and father still with us. Her hair used to curl after the rain and her skin, like Bridín's, glowed as the water on the bog at sunset. Even after all that'd happened, it was she alone I'd like to have seen. Who else could have understood me at that time?

Rose

The dwellings along the principal road and Church Lane were all re-roofed with the new tiles. Weekly, more people came to live in the town and the Governor's knights and soldiery swelled in number. Trade was good for all, and for three years Bridín and I produced respectable work that was well paid. Our outbuilding was always well stocked with wood and feed and we had enough coin for all that was needed. I knew I should have asked Bridín if she'd like to go to her mother in Kilkenny, but I never did and she never mentioned it.

'There's a dowry for you if you ever want to marry,' I told her.

She dismissed the idea.

'I might enter the nunnery, or I might stay as I am.'

She was young yet and I was in no hurry to lose her.

Without my mother or a husband to occupy my time, I took more interest in people. Cateline had another child, a boy who died in infancy, but her little one, Eve, gave us great joy. She tripped and fell upon the flags of our house but when Bridín played music she danced for us all. The husband of Cateline said he didn't like the child to spend too much time with us, for fear of our influence, but he was away a lot.

When Laurence O'Toole was finally canonised by Pope Honorius, people were divided in opinion but most in our area were pleased to have a saint, that hailed from a place so close to the town. In a strange crook of fate, his descendants were the very ones that the present Archbishop of Dublin was still fighting in the Wicklow mountains. In any case, his feast day was added to our calendar. Three days after

1326 – 1348

Martinmas, we honoured him and prayed to him for his intercession. My mother would have enjoyed the fuss that was made of one of her own although, within the family, he had been regarded as a saint in all but name for years. Brother James used every gathering as an excuse to preach about Saint Laurence O'Toole and said that he'd been blessed as a child with the holy water from the well at the back of the Abbey. This started a surge in the use of the well water and of the donations made by pilgrims.

Bridín had always been warned to stay well away from any man or boy who wanted to be alone with her. But a man with bad intent is craftier than a child. A mercenary at the barrack grabbed and held Bridín one morning as she was admiring the horses. His handling of her wasn't violent and she was too young to understand what he was doing. But when she told me of the mercenary, and of his strong grip and strange words, I was worried enough to speak with Sister Beatrice. At thirteen years, and with no father about, it was time to think about what might become of my beloved niece.

I asked her again about marriage but she said that she had seen what happened to women who had children and she had no desire to die that way.

'But all women who bring a child to life don't die; your mother lived after you were born.'

'Many do, and my mother isn't here any longer. Marriage sends people away to heaven or elsewhere.'

'In that case, Bridín, what about the nunnery?'

Rose

The sharp visitor of loss stuck in my chest. I wasn't ready to let the child go. But the nunnery was near and I could see her often.

'I suppose I can come home to see you?'

'I'll ask Sister Beatrice, she's always been good to us.'

I gave Bridín's dowry to the nunnery and I was glad to pay it. A young girl wasn't safe here and she seemed happy enough to go along with Sister Beatrice.

Stephen, the gravedigger, was a man of many guises. His first duty was the burial of the dead, but he also carried goods to the infirm in the town, and his cart was used to bring ailing people to the Priory. He was called on in times of emergency for he had an ability to organise people. It was a habit of his to preach at market day if he had something to say, or sometimes he'd preach about fornication, for devilment, just to goad Father Michael. Stephen would describe every detail of intimacy between a man and a woman or even between a man and a man. He had, on occasion, warned people about the practice of fornication with animals. He would talk at length about these matters and people would gather to hear it, jesting and cheering the more depraved he got. When he finished describing the acts, he would condemn them with great conviction, often just as Father Michael was about to put an end to it.

Stephen often stopped to talk to me and he brought with him the news and gossip he'd gathered as he worked. I always liked to see him.

No sooner had Bridín gone to Grane, than talk of raids and war began. Stephen's brother was a labourer on the land and kept the

Governor's sheep. He, along with the others who laboured on the plots, was expected to fight with the soldiers at times of trouble. They had been told to keep ready for war. Hunger was a weapon of war. At the mill, and everywhere that food was stored, soldiers were standing guard. Curfew was in place again and all the men of the town were obliged to keep watch with the guards.

Stephen had in his cart a sack of flour for Ava next door.

'The millers will always have bread, even if the rest of us starve.'

'Are you hungry, Stephen?'

He stood and patted his stomach,

'I have a great store of food in here,' he said. 'If you'd like it, I'll bring some later when it's ready.' He smiled at me, winked and made a farting noise. 'It's a shit pie. Similar taste to that of the baker's but at no cost of coin.'

He laughed at his joke and then told me of the trouble beyond the walls. I heard it myself later that night. When it was dark, the town was attacked. I sat by the fire, the door locked, afraid to go outside. Ava sent Geoffrey to get me. He was a fine young man by that time and apprenticed to his father. He was promised to a young woman.

'Come to our dwelling, Rose! It's not good to stay alone here; most of the town are below in the barn at the barrack.'

The Governor had ordered us there but I couldn't go into it. Even after the passing of time, the memory was as fresh as yesterday. I agreed to spend the night with Geoffrey and Ava. She was huddled at the fire with her small child. They were more afraid than I was, the Miller being in the thick of the battle.

Cries of anger and pain were to be heard, the slashing of metal in flesh, the clanging of swords, and arrows with burning tips were being shot over the wall. We were again thankful that the thatch was not in abundance. Ava remembered how it had burned the night the Bruces passed through. I told her how my people had seen the smoke and how much the burning of the town had saddened our family. The army of the Governor was better equipped but smaller in number. The wild Irish were brave but were not equally prepared. We waited in Ava's dwelling in dread of the victory of the raiders.

'Perhaps you will know the wild Irish and they won't kill you.'

'They will strike me down too Ava. I have no people beyond here anymore.'

We all looked the same to the foreigners. We prayed all night for the deliverance of the town and for Geoffrey, the miller.

Stephen was busy the next day. With the help of the men who were able, they brought all the bodies from the town to one place and laid them out. This was to try to identify those who had died. There were deaths on both sides, but more on the side of the wild Irish, who were left where they had fallen. The women would later try to recover their men. There was crying in the street as families realised their losses. It was a monstrous day. Ava's husband returned unharmed. Father Michael said Mass for all who'd lost their lives. There were over a dozen, and the grief of the town was uncontained. I attended the Mass and felt as if I alone stood out. I spent the next few weeks hiding lest anyone should accuse me of disloyalty. It grieved me to think of the bodies of the people strewn over the ground of the Governor because they had been fighting for food. It was also with sorrow that I remembered the people who were killed in protecting us. There must be a way we can live in peace; there would surely be enough to go around if we stopped fighting.

It was not rare for a place to be attacked more than once, so we were all uneasy over the following days. Cateline visited me and Stephen brought provisions. He was gentle in his talk and I was grateful for his and Ava's kindness. It eventually gave me the courage to venture out again. The other Irish people in the town felt the same as I did; we understood each other in ways that were beyond the reach of the townspeople.

I became accustomed in the passing of years to living alone. I was resigned to my empty dwelling, save for the cat, goat and hens. It was not without its advantages. People who came for garments often spoke of matters too close to speak of elsewhere. Ava asked if I'd teach her little one, Ismay, how to stitch. She was by this time seven and had a curiosity for learning. We passed many a mild hour working. When Bridín saw little Ismay sewing, she gave her the figurine that Cateline had brought so long ago and showed her how to cut and stitch clothing for it.

The nuns had sent Bridín on an intimate errand. When we lived in

Rose

the clan, my mother used to make undergarments that old Áine gave to expectant and nursing mothers, to alleviate the pain of swollen breasts. The underclothing was pleated, shaped and fastened to hold the extra weight. Eimear had continued to use them when she was in Grane and the nuns, who'd been given them, found them easier to wear than the linen that they wrapped around their chests. I was asked to make several of different sizes, and Bridín, who'd measured the women and bought the fabric at the market, was to stay and help me. It was easier work than the wedding gowns and paid just as well.

I had no desire to find another husband. There was no certainty that he would be sincere and no way of measuring the amount of good and evil in someone. I had no children but I accepted what God had taken from me and what He'd left in my possession. Health, straight limbs, nimble fingers, good eyes, a quick mind, coin enough for food and safe shelter. I had little to complain about. Music had returned to me and it was a kindly companion. On the feast of St Laurence O'Toole, ten winters after the death of my mother, I met a man who changed my mind about marrying again.

Brother James was standing at the well, using a cup to pour holy water into the vessels that people held out to him. It was a cold fresh day and it would be a colder night. A group of wild Irish was ahead of me; I spied instruments about them. When it came to their turn to receive the water, Brother James pointed at me and told them that I was one of their kind. I thought he meant that I was Irish like them, but he touched the harp that one of the men was carrying.

'The woman behind you is a piper; she's a great player but I never hear her play with anyone else. Perhaps she'll find you later for a tune.'

Embarrassed, I looked to the ground but one of the men asked me if I'd care to play with them and what tunes did I have and where did I come from.

'The tunes of the O'Byrnes,' I said.

The group bowed their heads and were silent for a time, for they'd remembered what'd happened.

'It's a fine thing that the tunes live on; we'll play them together this evening,' the harpist said.

I hadn't realised how much I had wanted to make music with others. I had never considered, until that moment, that it was a way of remembering my family.

After the blessings, prayers and offerings, we settled outside the Abbey in the walled garden, by a great fire, and the music lifted itself into the night, as sparks rose from the flames. No sooner had the harpist started to play the music and sing, than I fell under its spell. I taught them my father's favourite tunes and in turn I learned some new ones. When I heard the others play the music of my family, I cried. The harpist, whose name was Muiris, put a strong arm around me.

'It's to be expected; it's like hearing them beside you again,' he said.

We spent the whole cold night by the fire. It was as if the sadness in my heart had found a way out. The music knitted itself across the old wounds and they began to heal. It was as if I'd come home.

Rose

Muiris was thin; his bony cheeks protruded in his long handsome face. His nose was crooked as if once broken and he was tall. His eyes were green, with tiny yellow flecks that danced as he spoke. He seemed to know me. The familiarity was welcome. At the end of the night, as people drifted away or slept, I wanted to go back to my dwelling, but I didn't want to leave the musicians.

'Come with me; there's room enough to sleep there.'

Three of the group followed me – Muiris, Niall and Cathal. I was to learn that the three travelled throughout the land playing music. We spoke of life in our families and of the wars that had changed everything. They were O'Neills from the south. Their family name was known to me. They were not the warring O'Neills. Some of the tunes we played were slight variations of each other, a sign of good blood between us.

They stayed for a few days and, before they were due to move on, Muiris and I spoke of our marriages. He asked me why I had no children. I told him of Walter and of what had happened and I asked him if he were married and asked what had happened to his wife.

'It's a funny and a sad story, Rose, and I'll tell you how it happened. I had been away and returned to find her with the cock of my neighbour, a harpist from the west, in her mouth. It broke me at the time and every tune after that was tinged with sadness, no matter how much I tried to be rid of it. And then a funny thing happened. The people who heard my music said that it made them feel better, that the sound of sadness was a comfort to them. I can't explain why, but people said that it cured their sorrows. So now you have it, I can cure every broken heart apart from my own.'

He had restored my own heart, so I believed his words and I asked him where his wife was now.

'With the harpist, but they are welcome to each other. Those of my children who remain on this earth are young men now.'

Love doesn't use reason when it makes plans.

'If you want to stay a while in this dwelling, there's a place for you.'

Muiris gave up his wandering life and stayed from that day for twelve blissful years. We were wed and, to my utter delight, we were blessed with two children – a girl and a boy. I was given that which I'd believed I'd never have, and happiness was really ours for those years.

Not long after we were married, in the darkest part of the morning, a woman knocked at our door.

'Is the harpist in?' she asked.

I wondered if some ghost from the past had found us and was set to undo us. She was exhausted and wretched, her eyes red from crying, and she crumpled into the chair by the fire.

'They say he can cure a broken heart,' she said.

We invited her to stay and my husband played his harp and sang. The woman stayed through till morning, paid us and left with a lighter step. She was the first of a type of pilgrim that came to hear Muiris sing. Our dwelling became a place of music and companionship and was a sacred place to live.

Rose

Bridín was a welcome visitor and it was often on market day that she'd eat at our table. An evening in spring, on the feast of Saint Brighid, she brought sad news of her mother's death. Bridín had enquired about Eimear through a nun in Kilkenny. The Kilkenny nun had written back to Bridín, describing how Eimear had died in childbirth, and how the baby had gone the same way. It was a sad day for our family and we mourned our losses. Father Michael included them in his prayers for the whole month of February.

Rumours of pestilence were not uncommon but there were fears of many things at that time. There was no way of predicting which year would bring a bad harvest or sickness. The merchants were the first to speak of it; the news was brought to them from mariners. It was said that one ship drifted into the port of Waterford and that all on board, but a single man, had perished in the same manner: swellings upon the bodies and livid dark blotches over the skin. There were stories of whole families and entire towns dying, and the speed with which it struck was shocking. There were tales of hogs who had touched the clothing of the dead, dying. It was said that anything that touched the sick could communicate the malady to others.

We felt protected by the walls and by distance from the ports. It was common for the old people or the very young to become sick and be carried off. I had it in my mind that this was going to happen with the pestilence. Stephen spoke to me of it. He said that in some places the dead were reported to be left on the streets, and that he was thinking of asking the Governor to release the men to dig a pit for him.

1326 – 1348

It wasn't long before the rumours of pestilence in the land were confirmed. In the town of Dublin people were dying in great numbers. Tristledermot closed its gates, for we were on the trade route from Dublin to the south, and entry to strangers was denied. Market day was very quiet, only the usual traders could sell their goods. Masses were said at the Abbey and Saint James' Priory to pray for our protection and the deliverance of all those who'd died. Everyone was worried; some were so afraid that they locked themselves into their dwellings. Others made merry in the ale houses.

Muiris and I and the children carried on, wrapped in the warmth of our love and contentment, hoping that our town would avoid the fate of others. Deep down I was petrified by the stories. I knew that tragedy could move with stealth, and then rise like a monster in our midst to destroy everything dear.

My little one was nine summers by then and more beautiful with each fleeting day. She was like Bridín, who adored her, and fashioned for her a little habit with an apron, similar to her own. My son was named Niall after his uncle and he was the gentlest boy who ever lived, so like his father that it was as if they were the one person. His gift of music was equal to his father's, who said that one day his son would be the greatest harpist ever known. But life is indeed a strange son.

The first person to die from the pestilence was Stephen Scroope, a magistrate. Within days all our waiting was over and others quickly went the same way. We got word that the nuns in Grane had locked the nunnery and wouldn't be moving without nor admitting anyone. I

Rose

prayed for Bridín and for all the sisters. My little one, Evelin, asked me why she had to stay inside for entire days and I couldn't bring myself to tell her. Her brother told her that the *Luchtagairn* was roaming the town and we had to wait until the soldiery caught it and sent it back to its cave in Dunmore, the darkest place in the land.

'What does it look like? What does it eat?'

'It's a giant cat-like monster, and it eats children,' he said.

She was more afraid of this than she might have been of the pestilence. It kept her close to me and she didn't argue anymore about staying within our home. Stephen kept us informed of the spread of the disease in the town as he passed by, a body upon his cart. His lightness of spirit was still with him at that time. He would always stop, put down his cart and wink at me.

'You're looking well, Rose, compared to most.'

Although the sight of the dead person was dismaying, I was glad of his jesting. Who can live in the cesspit of terror without struggling to the surface for air? Without laughter, we would all drown.

Cateline and Eve never stopped visiting us through all the years I'd lived in the town. Cateline was as fine a woman as I'd ever met. She was kind to those who had little and always had good words that could grow hope even in the barest hearts. I'll never know how it was between her and her husband, but she was the best friend it was possible to have. She loved my family. Muiris changed his mind about foreigners through her. He was fond of both her and Eve, who had grown into a blossoming young woman.

1326 – 1348

When Cateline didn't visit us for two days, I knew something was wrong. Stephen told me of the pit the men had dug and he gossiped of strange cures.

'There's none that work, Rose.'

'What of Cateline?'

He looked to the ground and didn't need to say anymore. Within our dwelling I tried to make myself carefree but my husband, who could hear my voice even when I wasn't speaking, knew what had been said.

'Come, my love, we'll play our music together.'

The desolate wailing of grief became a familiar sound. One cold wet morning Stephen was passing, but his step was heavy and his shoulders were stooped. All in his brother's house were gone, his nieces, his nephews, all he loved were gone. He said that the woman who'd told him was dead too; she didn't get the boils, she died of grief, he said. It was the last time Stephen spoke. I saw him pass, but he didn't stop and didn't even look at me anymore.

It was deep winter, the pestilence had stayed as an unwelcome guest for weeks. My little one, Evelin, climbed into bed in the early morning, before the birds or cockerel had announced the start of a new day.

'I'm sick, Mam,' she said.

I held her into me; her little body was warm against mine. I kissed her fingers and stroked her hair.

'It's sore under my arm, Mam.'

She whimpered and I soothed her as best I could. I prayed to Saint Brighid, Saint Ita, to old Áine and to my mother that my little ones and

Rose

my husband wouldn't have to suffer for too long, and prayed that I'd keep breathing until they'd taken their last, so that I might comfort them.

Three days later, Evelin left this world and Niall and Muiris were close behind her. My prayers were answered and in the end all I could do was place my arms around them and pray. I didn't tell Stephen of their deaths; he would have guessed when he didn't see me at the door that we were afflicted. I waited for the pestilence to take me too and I would have been happy to go to my family, but for some reason I'll never know, I was spared.

Ava next door, and all belonging to her, perished. I couldn't let Stephen throw my beautiful family into the cold waiting mouth of the pit. As I was staring into the hearth, pulverised by grief, the thought came to my mind that I would travel to Kilkenny, to Diarmuid. I acted quickly, wrapped up a dress that I'd been working on for a wealthy woman in Moone, a winter dress. I'd wear it when I met him. I may well have been out of my mind but the thought visited me with such clarity that I had no choice but to obey it. It was like the voice of God speaking to me.

I laid my three jewels alongside one another and touched their faces for the last time. I poked the grate and built a fire until flames flickered high. I took the burning wood from the hearth and set fire to the bed where my family lay, resisting the urge to lie down with them. When the fire had taken hold, and the heat became intense, I put on my cloak, picked up the wrapped dress and walked away. It was easy to leave the town; there were no watchmen at the gate.

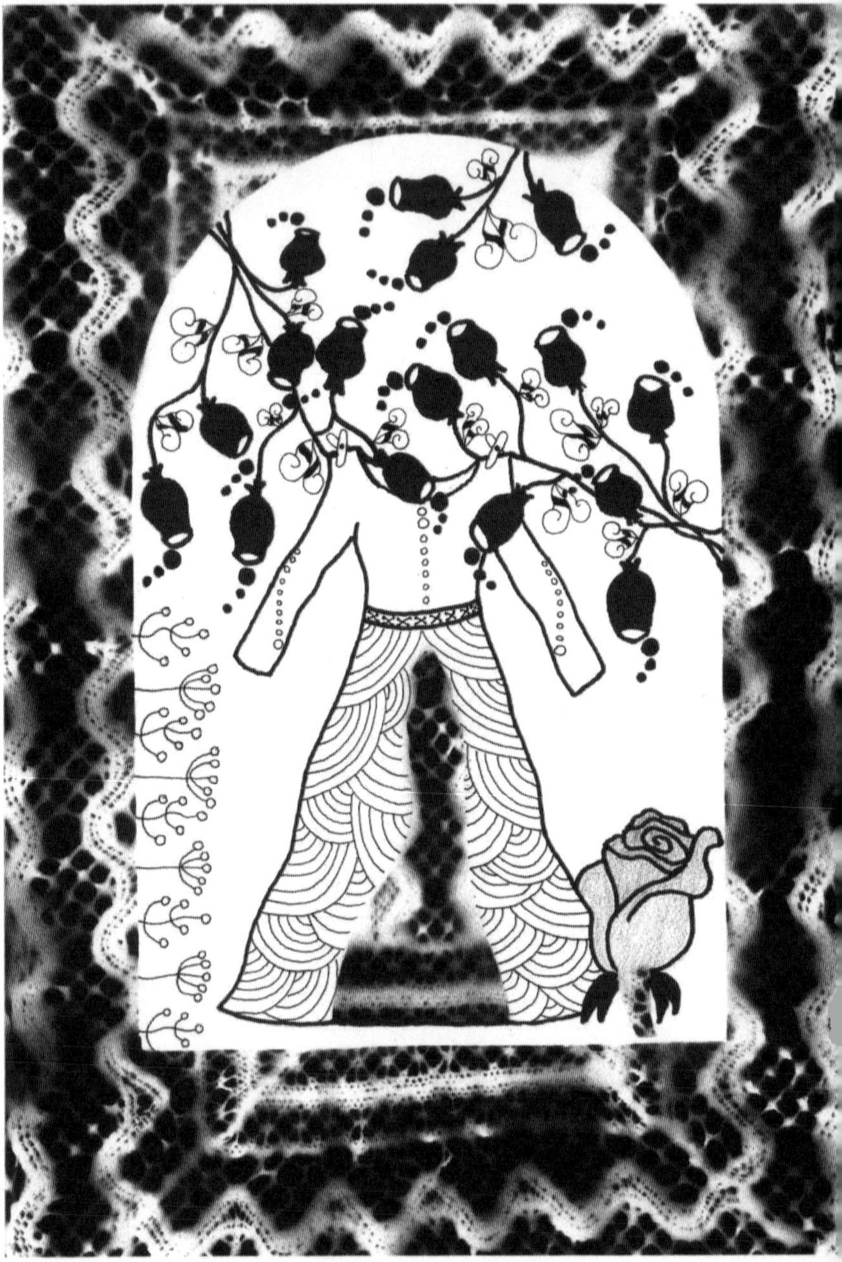

Chapter 14
Brother John and Rose
Wells and Kilkenny, 1348 - 1349

In the bristling cold hut, the monk and I are silent for a long time, lost in our thoughts. When he coughs it startles me. I forget what he asked me and it would seem he too has no memory of it. I know he can see that my heart is made of the ashes of grief, but he doesn't press me to explain why. Instead he hums another tune and makes a rhyme about me. It's funny indeed. He tells me that I remind him of a woman named Agnes and then his eyes fill with tears.

'I hope she was good-looking; my husband would pick a fight with you if you compared me to a crone.'

He smiles and my own tears fall. This life is a cruel master.

'Who is Agnes?'

He tells me of all he has lost and I ask him to hear my confession. I leave nothing out and then I say where I'm bound. He puts a heavy hand on my arm and tells me that I'll spend no time in purgatory, and that I have no need for penance, but that I'll go straight to my Lord and my family.

As the dawn opens the morning, we stand at the doorway.

'Have you ever seen colours more beautiful?' I ask him.

'Never,' he says, and then repeats himself as if making a promise to someone. 'Never.'

In the distance we see horsemen galloping, weapons glinting in the dawn light.

'The sheriff's men are coming to clear us all. If they know I've been to Tristledermot, they'll not spare me or anyone here.'

'Nobody goes into a town or out; fear has made hostages of us all.'

We gather our things and he goes out to warn the sleepy pilgrims.

'Rise up, rise up, the soldiery are coming towards us.'

People move slowly, stretching into wakefulness.

'Rise up!' he says again, 'and face this day, and the next with a good heart.'

I'm ready to go by the time he returns. He hands me his staff and then sits to write something on his parchment. He tears a piece and gives it to me.

'Pass this note to Brother John; he's one of the Black Friars in the Abbey in Kilkenny.'

'You'll have to read it to me, sir.'

'It's a note asking him to take care of you. I know him, he won't let you down.'

As we walk towards the road, away from the path of the soldiers, he places his warm hand upon my shoulder.

'I hope you find your stonemason, Rose, and I hope you marry. For the fifth time!'

'God speed you, sir,' I say and we part.

1348 - 1349

I arrive in Kilkenny; it is Christmas week in the year of Our Lord thirteen hundred and forty-eight. I set about looking for Diarmuid immediately. The note to Brother John has gained me entry to the town and given me a bed. Speaking to the woman who works in the kitchen of the Friary, I show her my dress and she tries it on.

'It's as warm as fleece,' she says and asks me to make one for her.

'As soon as I'm set up with my tools, I'll begin it.'

I leave her, and my dress, in the Abbey kitchen. I walk through the city, the sound of masons' hammers ringing in the air. The town is bigger than I had imagined and filthy. A market hall contains stalls of food and wares that are unusual to me. A man selling wolf skins tells me that the market is small in comparison to how it should be, on account of the rumours of pestilence. I ask him where I'll find the source of the hammering.

'All the masons are working at the new house on Rose Inn street.'

I smile at the mention of my name and wonder if the name reminds Diarmuid of me. At every turn I see the faces of my family in the features of strangers. I lower my eyes and move towards the sound. My feet are sore. In the distance a castle towers larger than any dwelling I've ever seen.

Through a gateway, I see a group of masons and carpenters standing. High up on a board held with rope, two masons are chiselling into the stone. A hammer falls from the hand of one.

'Below!' a voice shouts.

'Step back,' a man, who is standing close, says to me. He pauses.

'I'd recognise that wild mane anywhere.'

It's Diarmuid.

'And you, is it really yourself, Rose?

The light seems to shine from him as if independent of the sun. My legs are weak, I could fall. He seats me alongside himself on a low bench.

'You are like a vision. Tell me, is your mother still alive? Did you marry? You know that Eimear died in childbirth; she and the baby were buried together.'

I look up at the dwelling he is making.

'How can these buildings stand so tall? It's as if the earth has pushed them upwards. Could a man build a mountain if he so desired?'

'I can't believe you're here.'

The sound of hammering starts again. Diarmuid's eyes are dark and deep, but he's not Muiris.

'What's happened to you, Rose?'

'I don't know what I was thinking, coming here; I have nowhere else to go.'

My lip is trembling and my body shivering.

'You're freezing with the cold.'

He speaks with the men and then brings me to the home of his family. On the way we pass a fountain. I stop to drink, but he tells me that the water is bad. He has a well in the yard of his home. He never remarried after Eimear died. His brother and sister-in-law share their dwelling with him. I can't talk to them about the pestilence in

1348 - 1349

Tristledermot, although they've probably heard gossip about it. I can't speak of my family, I might die from the telling. They offer me their settle bed and I spend two dreamless days sleeping and several more resting and recovering.

I've been in Kilkenny for seven days. It's Christmas morning and we attend Mass. The bishop hasn't been seen in weeks for fear of the pestilence. After Mass, we hear that a Black Friar has died of the plague. He had the pus-filled boils and dark blotches on his skin.

'Perhaps it won't be as bad as we've heard,' Diarmuid's sister-in-law says. I don't tell her what's about to occur. There's no escaping the Black Death; I hope this time it takes me too. For some reason, I remember my winter dress and resolve to recover it from the Abbey.

In the weeks that follow, many more fall prey to the pestilence. The town is so big that it seems as if the world is ending and Judgement Day is coming. Among those taken is my very own stonemason, his rainbow heart dimming like the winter day.

There are no clergy to tend to the dying and none to give the last rites. We are abandoned. No bells or hammers ring out, the market hall is quiet. Animals roam looking for their masters. I alone remain in the dwelling of Diarmuid's family.

On the morning after the full moon in the New Year, I return to the Black Abbey. The winter dress is in the calefactory, upon the chair where I left it. My footsteps echo in the deserted corridors. There are no servants to be seen and no Black Friars. In the empty chapel I kneel to pray. They say that sorrow is passed down through families and that a person can go mad with the grief of their ancestors.

I pray for those who will come after me, that they may be given strength enough to carry their own losses, as well as those that have been passed to them. I pray too that they, like me, will always be given the courage to begin anew.

Acknowledgments

With special thanks to John MacKenna, Katie and Mairenn Jacques. Thanks, also, to Mark Turner; Faye Tucker; Magda Nowaksa; Dr Dolores MacKenna; Liz McColgan; Aoibhinn, Cillian and Lorcan Keogh; Dónal, Oisín, Clíodhna, Bronagh and Liadh Nolan; Matt, Brendan, Connor and Kiera Van Marter; Mary Lawler; Avril Winters; Castledermot Local History Society; Dermot Mulligan at Carlow Museum; Dr Margaret Murphy at Carlow College; Sara Donohue; Niamh Boyce; Christine Dwyer Hickey; Kevin Curran; The Irish Writers' Centre Novel Fair; Carlow Arts Office – Sinéad Dowling, Kelly Mooney and Aileen Nolan; Artl!nks; Frank Taaffe; Dr Sharon Greene and the work of Fin Dwyer.

A native of Kilkenny, Angela Keogh is a novelist, poet and playwright, living in Co Carlow. *The Winter Dress* was a winner at the Irish Writers' Centre Novel Fair 2020. Her stage plays have been toured by Mend & Makedo Theatre Co and her two most recent radio plays have been accepted by the Broadcasting Authority of Ireland for production in late 2020. She is a regular contributor to Sunday Miscellany on RTE Radio 1. Her poems have been published in a wide range of periodicals and have won a number of awards, including a Waterford Poetry Prize. She also works as an actor and theatre director.